Starting Over

Karen Tucci

DEDICATION

To my daughter Isabella, who

gave me a reason to write. I hope

one day you will have a passion for

literacy!

Contents

KAREN'S OTHER BOOKS:

Stand Alone Books:
<u>When the Dust Settles: A Sweet Romance with a Navy SEAL</u>

G & G Security Series (Coming 2025)
(The characters from When the Dust Settles cross-over in this series)
Operation: Heal my SEAL Book 1
Operation: Find my SEAL Book 2
Operation: Keep my SEAL Book 3
Operation: Train my SEAL Book 4

Second Chance Series:
<u>Starting Over</u>
<u>Moving On</u>

Big L' Ranch Series

The Perfect Kiss: Book 1

The Perfect: Cowboy Book 2

The Perfect Match Book 3

The Perfect Christmas (Holiday Novella)

The Perfect Sheriff Book 5

Best Friends Series

Let Me Carry You

Let Me Marry You

YA Cumberland Christian Prep School Series

The Big Score

CHAPTER 1

GUS GREENE WOKE UP bright and early Sunday morning with only one week to finish everything before his daughter and granddaughter arrived.

Since losing his wife, Gus neglected the housework and other renovations the property needed. He and his late wife always worked together to keep the house clean and orderly, but when Gus lost her, he let everything except his business go down. Now, he stayed one step above a slob by keeping his dishes and laundry washed and put away.

With Sarah moving back he felt alive. Not only would he have his daughter back and now his granddaughter, but he had a surprise for Sarah.

Gus arrived at church late, but he had an extra skip to his step, and people noticed.

"Good morning, Gus," Barbara greeted him at the door. "You look happy this morning."

"Morning doctor. My daughter will be home soon," Gus whispered excitedly, since Pastor Pete had already started the music.

Gus noticed Barbara's usual lavender scent, noticeably sweeter today. Realizing that he was staring at Barbara with adoration, Gus grabbed a bulletin off the wooden table, and headed to a pew in the middle of the overheated sanctuary to read the announcements.

Gus was so eager for his daughter's return that he struggled to focus on the pastor's sermon. The August heatwave they were having didn't help his ability to concentrate, either.

That shifted when Gus heard Pastor Pete Knight ask for praises and prayers from the congregation.

Gus, a sixty-year-old with thinning silver hair and a five o'clock shadow already covering his round face, bolted upright from his pew. His excitement forced everyone to turn in his direction.

"Sarah and Lily are coming home. They should be here next Sunday. I would appreciate it if everyone could pray for traveling mercies. Having an entire congregation praying for them eases my heart."

As a devout Christian, Gus had always acknowledged that the Lord God Almighty looked over and protected all His children.

"Marlene is looking after them, too," Miss Clancy said, as Gus sat back down.

"I believe that, too."

The mention of his love tugged him back to last winter. Marlene died during a January snowmobile ride. Not fond of riding over water, Marlene hammered on the snowmobile throttle to get across the pond. She rocketed into the air after hitting a ridge at sixty-five miles per hour. She landed facedown on the ice, and the machine landed on top of her, pinning her lifeless body to the frozen water. Gus, Pastor Pete, and Pearle, the Pastor's wife, freed her from underneath the sled, but she died upon impact.

"We will definitely pray for their safe arrival, and hopefully, they will join us here on Sundays," Pastor Pete encouraged.

After the service ended, people mingled in the sanctuary. They made plans for the upcoming week and shared news from the past week. Pastor Pete faithfully waited at the exit to say bye to each person—sometimes taking an hour or more.

"Gus, got a minute?" Brandon's deep voice echoed from across the sanctuary. As he reached Gus, he asked, "When do you want me to look at your list of repairs?"

"Funny you should ask," Gus said slyly. "I was hoping you would wait a week until Sarah arrived. I'd like you to meet her."

"What are you trying to manipulate, Old Man?" Brandon was the only person on the planet allowed to call Gus Old Man. Brandon and his dad, Caleb, restored parts of Gus's property for the past six years.

Gus pulled out his wallet and showed Brandon the picture of Sarah that she sent him last year. "Who me? I'm not up to anything. I just think you two should meet." Gus shrugged. "I mean, she should have some say in the repairs since she'll be living with me," he added with a smile.

"Even though I don't believe you, I am quite busy wrapping things up for other clients, so how does the first week of September sound?" Brandon replied.

"Perfect. I'll be counting the days," Gus said as he glided toward the exit.

Brandon hollered, "Don't set me up, Gus."

With a wave of his hand, Gus dismissed Brandon's demand.

Out in the parking lot, Jill Jamieson stopped Gus. "Mr. Greene, do you think Sarah and Lily will be up to having company when they arrive? Jerry and I were hoping to stop by with the kids."

"Jill, I am not your Sunday School teacher anymore. Please call me Gus. As for visiting Sarah, I would give her a few days to settle in. I know Lily is not happy about moving here, and honestly, I don't know how Sarah feels about the move, so I think they will need an adjustment period. I will do everything I can to get her to church."

"I hope so." Jill frowned. "Apologizing for how I treated Sarah during our senior year is really important."

Jill and her husband, Jerry, graduated from high school with Sarah and her late husband, Jake, but Jill's better-than-everyone-else attitude irritated Sarah.

Gus spent many nights helping Sarah navigate her growing frustration, especially when Jerry started dating Jill. Eventually, Sarah and Jerry stopped being close friends.

His eyes crinkled when he smiled. "You'll have your chance. Give her time."

They said their goodbyes, and as Gus drove home, he prayed aloud.

"Lord, you've watched over Sarah since she got accepted to the University of Florida at Gainesville and left with Jake. You blessed them with a wonderful marriage and a beautiful little girl. Please, give me the wisdom I need to help them both feel at home here, amen."

Gus would be devastated if he botched this. Instead of being blunt with Sarah about her need to start over, he crafted a plan that would be impossible for her to ignore.

CHAPTER 2

As they reached the Maine state line, Sarah Morris realized that the weather had changed little since she left. Maine's humid August weather couldn't compare to *real* humidity in Florida that Sarah longed for. It had only been a little over a day since she'd left the Sunshine State, and she missed it already.

Sarah turned off the air conditioner in her Honda Pilot and pressed the button for the power windows. She'd embraced this weather, for in a few short months, the dreaded Maine winter would overcome her.

The hot breeze blew a streak of Sarah's blonde hair over her eyes. Sarah quickly stuffed the loose strand in her messy bun so it wouldn't distract her. Sarah's muscle-defined legs yearned for a stretch. After the long drive, Sarah couldn't wait to go for one of her runs. The sound of her feet hitting the pavement always made her feel better.

"We'll be at Grandpa's in about an hour. Are you all set, or should I stop somewhere?" she shouted so Lily would hear her over the music blaring from her iPod and the wind. Driving from Florida was a feat, especially with only one driver. Sarah was proud of herself, though, since the trip up the East Coast only took her a day and a half.

"Whatever, I don't even want to be here!" Lily snapped. "We never should have left Florida, so do whatever you want and leave me out of it, like you did when you decided to move here!"

Sarah couldn't believe how much their relationship had changed since Jake died. With a heavy heart, she thought back to the way life used to be. They spent weekends traveling Florida's coastline, playing board games, laughing endlessly, and forging a bond Sarah never thought would be broken. One thing they had enjoyed together was running, but that, too, had stopped.

Ever since Lily could stand on her own, she ran with her parents. Just last year, the three of them ran the half-marathon and marathon at Walt Disney World. Sarah regretted running ahead of Jake and Lily to qualify for the Boston Marathon because she didn't end up racing after Jake's death. Sarah wondered if she would get back her entire relationship with Lily one day.

After fifty minutes of driving, Sarah neared her dad's home. The woods adjacent to the acres of farmland that Sarah played on as a child were replaced with complexes, family homes, and stores.

The one thing Sarah enjoyed most about Maine was gone. *Where did the kids play?* Sarah wondered.

However, having more houses might mean there were kids Lily's age, and she could make friends quickly and forgive me for uprooting her life. If not, Lily would meet people at school in two weeks, when the year began.

Sarah jolted out of her thoughts when a squirrel scrambled back and forth in the street. Fortunately, Sarah stopped quickly—within an inch of the squirrel's life.

As Sarah pulled into the driveway, she couldn't help but notice how bad her dad's store looked. *How could Dad entice people to buy his vegetables from that store?* Sarah silently critiqued.

Chipped paint and split boards hid the store's rustic charm. Water stains marked the store's outside wall. The roof shingles needed to be replaced. Marlene had always taken extra care of the walkway, made sure it bloomed with flowers to welcome the customers; not Gus. The rock wall parallel to the store's walkway needed to be realigned. Remembering the brutal Maine winters, with their bone-chilling temperatures and freezing rain, Sarah concluded they'd destroyed the wall.

"I'll have to encourage Dad to get that contractor he raves about to fix up the store as nicely as he fixed up the house," Sarah said aloud.

Last year, Sarah's parents finally put up royal blue shutters to complement their light blue colonial. It pleased Sarah to see the vinyl siding that they put up with the shutters. As her dad aged, easy house maintenance was a necessity.

Sarah fondly remembered lying on the roof of the farmer's porch in the summer, gazing at the stars and asking God to show her the future. She never thought she would be a motherless widow at thirty-four, returning to her parents' home.

Seeing Gus scurrying from the house brought Sarah back to reality. She whipped off her seat belt and pushed the car door open.

Sarah ordered Lily out of the car. Lily grumbled as she dragged herself out of her seat.

"I can't believe how grown-up you look," Gus crooned over his granddaughter.

While the teen rummaged through the trunk, Gus whispered to his daughter. "What's up with the skimpy top and way too snug shorts?"

"She's fully covered, Dad."

"She will need a father figure to watch over her," Gus mumbled, making his way toward Lily.

Thanks, Dad. I can take care of myself and my daughter. You needed help, remember?

Embracing Lily, he said, "You've grown so tall. Ah, you remind me of your dad. I'm so glad to see you! I have a room all ready for you."

Lily bolted back in the car, slamming the door shut. Gus gazed at Sarah, a sad expression marking his face. Before he could express his apology, Sarah put her hand on her dad's shoulder and told him to keep that topic off-limits for a while.

Gus entered the backseat of the car from the passenger side. "I'm so incredibly sorry, Lily," he said, his voice thick with regret. "Please believe me, it was unintentional that I upset you; I hope you can forgive me."

"Hi, Grandpa. I'm not excited about being here. I don't see why you couldn't move to Florida. There's only one of you, and there's two of us. Plus, I have—correction—had friends there."

Gus quickly recognized Lily's sharp tone. "You sound just like your mother when she was your age. I survived her, and I bet I'll do better the second time around," Gus laughed as he helped Lily out of the car.

"Sorry, Dad."

Gus gave his daughter a lingering hug and kiss on the cheek, and as he held her, Gus whispered, "It will be okay."

He released her and announced, "It's still early. Why don't you girls clean up and go to church with me? I've been telling everyone that you'd be home today. They can't wait to see you two." Without breathing, Gus rambled on with his next thought. "Sarah, I talked to my friend, Jim. He's a principal at the middle school in town, and though he doesn't have any openings for a teacher this year, he said you should volunteer or substitute, which might open doors for next year at the new school."

"New school?"

"Yeah, Brookwater School got too small, so we had to build a bigger one a few miles away," Gus explained.

Sarah's heart stopped as her mind raced. *New School. Next year. I want to teach this year. If I don't teach, I'll have too much time on my hands to think, and that is overrated.*

Gus jolted her from her thoughts. "Honey, I'll get your bags. What about church?"

Sarah hesitated while her dad hustled to the trunk. *The last thing I want to do is return to church. Jake and I left the snobby, know-it-alls behind sixteen years ago, but Dad never gives up.*

Sarah grabbed the duffle bag from the back seat. "I don't think either of us is up to going to church today. We need to clean up and rest. Maybe Lily and I will go next Sunday." The last thing Sarah wanted to do was give her dad something to hold over her head, but the insinuation that she would join him next week just slipped out of her mouth.

Lily barely turned before she shouted, "Speak for yourself! I have to live here, but I don't have to like it by participating in anything other than going to school." Sarah and Lily agreed that school was a priority.

Lily stormed into the house while Gus put his arm around his daughter's shoulders with a smile and led her into the house. "Welcome home, honey. I've missed you so much."

She'd missed her dad, too. But she was afraid this might be the worst decision she'd ever made!

CHAPTER 3

TWO WEEKS DISAPPEARED. SARAH felt restless and discouraged. Movers broke some of her furniture, and though responsible for anything broken or destroyed, the hassle of dealing with them grated on Sarah's nerves.

Once she finished dealing with one problem, another one popped up.

Lily stomped down the stairs and stopped on the landing. With her hand on her hip, she didn't wait for her mother to acknowledge her. "Why do we have to live here? Why couldn't we just visit and go home?"

"What about Grandpa?" Sarah asked with concern. "He needs us here to help him with the store and everyday life," Sarah added.

Tears ran down Lily's face, and she snapped at her mom, "I lost someone too. It's not all about you adults losing people." As Sarah moved toward the stairs to console her daughter, Lily turned and ran back up, skipping two stairs at a time. Feeling empty and defeated, Sarah fell to her knees and sobbed.

Gus returned from his store and stopped short as he saw Sarah curled up in tears. Without saying a word, Gus wrapped his arms around his daughter and let her cry.

Sounding drained, "It's been a week; I don't think I can do this, Dad!"

Despite her anxious thoughts stealing her sleep, the next morning Sarah accompanied her dad to church, while Lily stayed home.

Gus introduced Sarah to everyone he could, making it too difficult for Sarah to remember names. They commented on how much she looked like Marlene and offered their sympathies for her losses.

The most genuine woman looked sixty-ish. Her blue eyes, covered by glasses, shone brightly when she talked about Marlene.

Jill grabbed Sarah's arm and gave her a big hug and kiss on the cheek. An overwhelming sense of dread poked Sarah in the chest. It left her feeling trapped, suffocated by her past. *You were mean to me in high school, so why are you acting like my best friend now?*

"I asked God to give me a close friend to share life, and it looks like He answered my prayers."

Sarah glanced left, then right. *Is she talking about me? The one she tormented in high school. I don't think so.*

Free from her past frenemy, Sarah sat down in the pew next to her dad and inquired about the lady with the blue eyes.

"That's Miss Clancy. She and your mom were best friends." Sarah could have guessed. Her mom was friends with the nicest people.

While Pastor Pete delivered his sermon, Sarah spent half of her time listening and half observing the people in the congregation. Her eyes had kept landing on this man in the second pew who never took his eyes off Pastor. At appropriate times, he raised his hand and called out, "Amen."

Sarah couldn't deny his flowing, dark hair, broad shoulders, and rippling muscles. She figured he must be over six feet tall, given how much of his back she saw above the pew. Sarah felt guilty for thinking this man was incredibly handsome, or as Lily would say, eye candy, but his looks were undeniably the best she had ever seen since Jake.

When the pastor finished his sermon, Sarah watched her dad hug almost everyone in the church as she tried to make herself invisible. To no avail, Jill cornered her and refused to let her leave until Sarah agreed to get together soon. Jerry, her husband, and once loyal elementary friend, embraced Sarah with the strength of ten men.

Sarah and Jerry lost touch as they went through adolescence. In high school, they stopped speaking all together when Jerry began dating Jill. She was the snobbiest, rudest girl in school. Sarah lost all respect for Jerry and never understood why he would be with someone like that.

"Sarah, it's been so long. Jill and I were thrilled when we heard you were moving back. I'm really sorry to hear about Jake, though." As Jerry tried to place his hand on Sarah's elbow, Sarah pretended she had an itch on her shoulder and moved her arm away. "When do I get to meet your daughter?"

"Yeah, when can we meet her? Our twins, Joseph and Jenny, can't wait. They're fifteen, too."

Thoughts of Lily being home alone made Sarah smile because she had a reason to leave. "Actually, she's home right now, so I should get back to her. I'm sure you'll meet her soon. It was nice to see you guys." Sarah excused herself and corralled her dad out the door.

"I wanted to introduce you to someone, but he must have left already," Gus said disappointedly.

"Well, maybe you can introduce me next week," Sarah replied.

"Oh, you bet I will."

CHAPTER 4

LILY STARTED SCHOOL TOMORROW, but her demeanor had remained mostly unchanged. Even though the teen yelled less, Sarah thought her daughter was akin to a prickly cactus.

"Do you mind if I go for a run?" Sarah dragged herself outside to her dad's shop. Lacking motivation, she needed to clear her head and work her body.

She'd replenished the vegetable bins yesterday. Now, they sat waiting for his loyal clientele from church, who arrived after service each week to purchase their produce.

"Are you okay, honey?" Gus removed his gardening gloves. "There's someone I want you to meet."

Her dad had already mentioned introducing Sarah to Brandon, his contractor. *I'm not interested in dating.*

"Dad, don't set me up with anyone, please."

He ignored her plea and urged his daughter to greet the first customer.

"Hi, Sarah." Pastor Pete strolled toward the store. "Your dad told me about the difficult times happening with Lily."

Overwhelmed by emotions, Sarah's eyes welled up with tears. "Hopefully, it will get better soon. Thank you for your sermons." Sarah listened to previous ones on the church website since her first visit. "One helped me reach Lily," Sarah said with sincere appreciation.

"God knows what His people need. It's just my job to listen to Him and say what He tells me," Pastor Pete said humbly.

Pray tell, what do I need? Sarah asked silently.

"If you ever want to talk, call me or stop by. Everything will be okay, eventually. God works through all of us."

"Thank you."

Miss Clancy and Grammie Glenice pulled in next. The latter earned her name from the congregation by donating her time to the nursery during the service.

When they exited the car, Sarah spoke loud enough for them to hear.

"My dad is inside the store. I'll see you soon, Pastor."

She jogged toward the women. "Hi, ladies. My dad will help you today. I need to move this body."

"Do it while you can. When you get our age, this is the extent of physical activity," Miss Clancy joked.

They shared a laugh as Sarah ran off.

With music blaring from her iPhone into her headphones, she began the mile stretch down her road and remembered the best part of running with Jake. He encouraged and pushed Sarah to meet her running goals and guided Lily through extensive training for her marathon. Sarah didn't care that she had qualified for Boston, but never participated.

As thoughts and tears overwhelmed her, she ran harder and faster and tried to clear her head, but couldn't. Her thoughts, mostly regret, consumed her.

Lily doesn't want to be in Maine. I don't either; winter is coming, which means my road running will end. Plus, I miss teaching in Florida. Dad needs me. Sarah reminded herself, trying to convince herself that she needed to be in Maine.

It's been almost a year since her Mom died, and she didn't want Dad to be alone. Did she want to face Jake's one-year anniversary on her own? No. She knew she'd be a mess.

Sarah's run spurred her thinking. If she stayed here could she replicate her childhood for Lily? Would Lily want her to?

Like Lily, Sarah was an only child and had all her parents' attention. They made scarecrows, carved pumpkins, swam in Sebago Lake, went to the animal park and Fun Spot, the best theme park in the state. Now they have Adventure Park, an adrenaline junkies dream full of zip lines and rope courses. Sarah hoped Lily would want to do these things because she wanted to, and doing them alone didn't sound fun.

Running faster, Sarah's knee twitched, but she ignored the quick shooting pain, hoping it would just go away.

She continued to let her thoughts overrule the pain. *I'll never be as good of a mom to Lily as my mom was to me.*

Did she want to move back to Florida and risk missing out on time with her dad, like she missed the last sixteen years with her mom? No.

How could she make Lily see that true love meant sacrificing things one loves?

With tears falling from her cheeks, Sarah pushed herself to run faster, forgetting her knee pain. As her right foot pounded the pavement, her legs buckled, and she fell, sliding on the blacktop with her arms straight out in front of her, just like Pedroia would slide onto home plate.

In total shock, Sarah sat up, rested her elbows on her knees, cradled her head in the palm of her skinned hands while her tears pooled before they ran down her wrist. She lifted her shirt and checked her stomach. There, she found the worst road rash she had ever seen.

Sarah squeezed her knee until her fingers turned white. Enough pressure should ease the pain.

Dread knotted in her stomach when she heard runner's feet pounding the pavement and heavy, though controlled, breathing behind her.

She knew it was a skilled runner and her cheeks grew red hot with embarrassment when she pushed off the ground and fell back down, unable to bear weight on her knee.

"Are you okay?" The runner asked as he stopped to assist Sarah.

She looked up and saw the same attractive man from church. *Are you kidding me—not my finest hour to be meeting him,* Sarah thought silently.

Her pulse hammered against her ribs, a frantic plea to her Father above that this be a dream.

A wave of surprise washed over Sarah as she saw the man extend his hand, his presence sparking an unexpected surge of excitement.

"I am fine, just truly embarrassed. I guess it doesn't matter how long you are a runner, a bad knee will get you every time," Sarah joked.

"You're Gus's daughter, right?" He inquired.

She smiled and shook her head. "My name is Sarah." She didn't allow him a chance to respond before she continued, "I've seen you in church, but I'm sorry, I don't know your name."

"It's Brandon Taylor. I am heading to your dad's house now to plan my day for tomorrow."

This is him? Feeling even more embarrassed, with this handsome man eyeing her every move, Sarah pushed onto her feet. What would she do if she couldn't walk? She'd crawl if necessary. "Thanks for stopping to check on me, but I'm fine. Please continue your run."

Brandon wrapped an arm around Sarah's waist, and he placed her arm around his neck.

"Excuse you. Do you make a habit of invading people's space?" This close, Sarah felt the warmth of his body and an uncomfortable tingle spread through her.

Sarah jerked away, wincing when her weight pressed down on her ankle. These weren't feelings she wanted any part of. "I'll be okay. I can do it on my own."

"I don't mind the interruption and it doesn't look like you'll be home before Christmas if I don't help you," Brandon said with a hearty laugh.

Sarah hoped he didn't notice her phony laugh in response to his joke. She reluctantly agreed to his help. But her eyes widened when he scooped her up in a bridal style.

"What are you doing?" She demanded with a shriek.

"Taking you home."

They passed seven mailboxes, as he discussed his ambitious business goal of extending his clientele, and his participation in church without becoming winded.

His closeness sent sensations zinging through her body that she worked hard to ignore. One word came to mind as her body drew him in—betrayal. She shouldn't feel this way. What would Jake say?

As if he could read her mind, he offered condolences. "I'm really sorry about your losses. I can't imagine losing a parent and a spouse so close together."

"Thank you." What else could she say?

For the first time, Brandon sucked in a breath. "Put me down, please. We're almost home."

"I've got you. If you question my manhood again, I'll throw you over my shoulder and carry you the rest of the way caveman style."

She had no idea why that sounded so intriguing. This man had already topped the charts on protective appeal, and it scared her to death.

Drowning in unwanted emotions, Sarah felt a wave of relief when the sight of her dad's fence interrupted the awkward moment.

"What happened?" Gus asked when Brandon brought Sarah into the house and set her on the couch.

"She fell. Good thing I was there. She can't put any weight down on it."

Sarah's head bobbed back and forth between the men speaking about her as if she wasn't in the room.

"Hello, I'm right here. I can speak for myself."

They both stared at her, but she had nothing else to say, so she stacked up pillows and propped her leg up.

"Thank you, Brandon, for helping my daughter home. I'll meet you outside and we can discuss winterizing the greenhouse and the other jobs I have in mind."

Brandon smiled at Sarah. She should have refrained from returning it, but he had a way of pulling her in closer.

"So, you met my handyman?" Gus asked in a high-pitched voice. Sarah grunted, not giving him the satisfaction of an answer. "You can't tell me you don't think Brandon's attractive."

Sarah ignored her dad's question and asked him to get her an ice pack.

Handing it over, Gus said, "I'll be in the store. If you need anything holler, I should hear you, but if I don't, I'm sure Brandon will," Gus joked.

"Funny Dad. You're getting on my last nerve."

No other man besides Jake had ever evoked the intense feelings Brandon ignited in her during that walk. It had to be a direct link to her pain, right?

A bitter laugh escaped Sarah. Maybe Lily was right—moving here was a terrible mistake.

Chapter 5

At thirty-five, Brandon Taylor inherited the construction business from his dad, who retired early so he could travel with Evelyn, Brandon's mom.

Though he had maintained his dad's clients and upheld the workmanship quality, Brandon wanted more. The desire to prove to his dad that he was reliable and could expand the business.

Brandon wondered if his father had any faith in him at all and often questioned why his dad gave him ownership of his most prized possession.

Gus treated Brandon more like a son than Caleb did. The thought intrigued Brandon. Since meeting Sarah, she had consumed his mind. He could still feel her soft blonde hair tickling his bare forearms and a sharp zing in his chest whenever he saw her.

"Come on!" Brandon let the measuring tape snap back into its holder. He measured the same side of the greenhouse three times and recorded three different measurements.

He ran his fingers through his hair and sighed.

"What's the problem?" Gus chortled, the man's evil ways clear. He knew full well "his problem" had wavy blonde hair, a slender runner's body, and a busted knee.

Brandon reprimanded himself for taking over like the caveman he threatened to be, and carrying Sarah home. Not only did he make her uncomfortable, but he's been unable to function normally since.

Gus probably didn't want to hear his thoughts. Brandon hadn't been prepared for the feel of Sarah's body against his. She had equal parts of tone muscle and soft flesh.

When he recalled the feeling of electricity that shook his body, the image of *Christmas Vacation*, where Chevy Chase's entire body was lit up, came to mind.

"Nothing. Just distracted." As soon as he said it, Brandon knew he'd said too much.

"Is she as distracted with you?"

"Doubtful."

"Want me to go ask?"

Brandon slapped his hand against his thigh. "No! This isn't high school, Gus. I have to focus on my work."

He couldn't let a beautiful woman pull him from his goal of having a successful business. Not if he didn't want his dad criticizing him.

Rather than make it a big deal, Brandon returned to his work. Meanwhile, Gus walked away, yelling over his shoulder. "Meet me in the store in five minutes."

Ten minutes later, he found Gus at the workstation, bundling and canning his veggies. "What took you so long?" Gus chuckled.

Not waiting for an answer, Gus kicked another chair Brandon's way, so he took a load off. "You can't get good help nowadays," he muttered, probably trying to entice Brandon into a conversation.

When that didn't work, he blurted, "You saved my daughter. That's interesting."

"How so?"

Brandon picked up a handful of green beans and popped them into his mouth, hopeful he wouldn't say anything incriminating.

"Hey, hey, don't eat all my profit. I have to get money to pay you somehow," Gus joked.

"I can't help it. I've never tasted better green beans," Brandon smiled as he shrugged.

"You can't stop God's will." Gus stated.

Brandon pushed out a short breath mixed with a light laugh. "You can't force God's will either," Brandon countered.

"Semantics."

While shoveling green beans in his mouth, Brandon tilted his head, listening for a voice he thought he heard.

"Dad, where are you?" Sarah hollered.

"You already know the sound of her voice," Gus said in a sly tone.

Brandon would be smart to pack up his tools and speed away before his heart got any ideas.

CHAPTER 6

SARAH SPRANG UP IN bed the next morning, soaked in sweat from a nightmare about Lily's first day. A flash of understanding brought a sense of apprehension.

An icy river spread through her veins as she realized why Lily was upset about starting over. She felt betrayed by Sarah and that clawed at her heart.

Besides her friends and the only home she'd ever known, Lily left behind a basketball opportunity. At the end of last season, Lily's former coach told Lily she'd move her to the varsity team and make her co-captain.

As she climbed out of bed, Sarah asked God for help again. A surge of hope filled her to the brim. Lily could earn a spot on the varsity basketball team. Would she try?

It didn't take much to get Lily in a morning tizzy. She required a lot of sleep, but sleep deprivation was not the cause of this morning's predicament. The bane of Sarah's existence and moving to Maine were still her top problems, but the morning's dilemma was what to wear on the first day of school.

"You look beautiful, Lily," Sarah insisted as she rushed into Lily's room. With her tall and toned frame, Lily could wear a bathrobe and be beautiful. Her bright pink theme park shirt looked perfect with her blonde hair and fair skin. Her worn jeans kept the look casual. "Hurry! You'll be late for the bus," Sarah urged.

"Mom, you just don't understand. It took sixteen years for me to fit in with my friends and earn a place in sports—I don't have any of that here!"

Sarah knew Lily was referring to her best friend, Mikala, whom she started kindergarten with and has stayed very close to ever since. "Your abilities haven't changed. You are beautiful, and you've got a great personality; stop worrying," Sarah tried to assure her daughter.

"Thanks, Mom. Every girl just loves to hear that," Lily retorted as she rushed by her mom and ran downstairs.

Running out of time, Lily grabbed a breakfast bar and ran to the bus. Presumably still upset with her mom, Lily ignored Sarah's request for a kiss or a hug—Sarah would have settled for either.

"Since the kids are in school, I have some time right now to come over and catch up if you're not busy," Jill declared, making Sarah cringe.

Silence filled the phone. Unable to think of an excuse to prevent this from happening, Sarah finally told Jill the truth. "I hurt my knee on a run yesterday and I'm in a lot of pain. Plus, I have to help my dad in the store."

Sounding concerned for Sarah, Jill asked, "Are you okay?" She didn't let Sarah answer the question before she asked another one. "How did you get home?"

"Brandon Taylor stopped while I was sitting on the ground. He brought me home." Sarah left out that he held her close to his chest as he carried her the entire way.

"Lucky you. Brandon is a looker. He's an eligible bachelor, you know?" Jill encouraged.

Exasperated, Sarah replied, "Seriously. I'm all set. I am not interested in dating anyone," Sarah assured Jill.

As if he knew Sarah mentioned his name, Brandon's truck pulled into the driveway.

Jill wasn't one to give up until she got her way. "Hey, someone just pulled in. Maybe we can get together soon when I'm feeling better. I'll talk to you later."

What made Jill think Sarah would hang out? Jill spent her last year in high school insulting Sarah for focusing on basketball. During the state championship basketball game, Sarah scored thirty points and had seventeen assists. After winning the championship, Jill neglected to congratulate her. Instead, she criticized Sarah for the shots she missed.

Sarah shuffled to the door and then opened it halfway. "Good morning."

"How's the knee this morning?" Brandon asked, his voice deep and alluring.

"Better than yesterday." Her eyes roamed over his flannel shirt, covering his broad shoulders.

She shouldn't be looking at him like that, so she backed up, creating necessary distance between them. Then her words proved her a liar when her knee buckled and Brandon's arm wrapped around her hip. "Whoa there."

She relished the feeling of his strong forearms underneath her fingers. Her gaze fell to his hands, which felt in too intimate of a spot for having just met. Though carrying Sarah home flush to his rippled chest wasn't any less affection.

Despite the warmth blooming in Sarah's chest, she hopped back and Brandon's hands fell to his sides. A fleeting look of disappointment crossed his features before he hid it.

"I won't keep you from what you're doing, but I came to offer you a proposition."

CHAPTER 7

SARAH'S PRESENCE AND BEAUTY made her a constant distraction! It'd been a week since Brandon began working at Gus's. The unusually warm September heat beat down on his bareback, while his mind raced.

What would it take to change Sarah's mind about him?

He descended each ladder rung until his feet hit the ground. Brandon pulled a water bottle from the cooler in his truck and guzzled it just as Lily pulled into the driveway.

"Hi, you must be Lily. Your Grandpa told me all about you."

Lily placed her hand on her hip and curled her lip. "And you are?"

"Brandon Taylor. I am renovating this place for Gus. What do you think so far?" Brandon inquired. Why did he care what a teenager thought? Because she was Sarah's daughter. The answer made his insides squirm.

With a quick tilt of her head and rock of her upper body, Lily retorted, "If I could tell what you did, I'd let you know if I liked it, but it doesn't look like you've done any work yet."

"Mother like daughter," he mumbled as Lily stormed away.

"Mom, Grandpa, I'm home!" Lily yelled.

Needing to speak with Gus, Brandon followed behind her.

"We're back here, Lily."

When they reached the backroom, he spied Sarah in a chair with her leg propped up, peeling vegetables, while Gus worked at the stove.

Sarah dropped the green bean from her hand; her gaze lingering on Brandon's upper body. Her reaction caused a wave of heat to swirl in his chest.

She'd rejected Brandon's offer to reunite her with her home state. Based on the way she stared at him, it gave him a little relief that her rejection wasn't personal.

Gus cleared his throat, drawing Lily's attention to the connection between her mom and Brandon.

There were daggers in the girl's eyes when she said, "Hmm. That's how you used to look at *Dad*."

"Lily, you're out of line—"

"Whatever, Mom, I did my job today—school—"

"Don't be rude," Sarah ordered. "Did you have a bad day?"

Brandon felt out of place and exposed. The lack of his shirt, only slightly responsible. He understood fighting with a parent. His dad and him argued all the time about putting customers first, and building the business.

But Sarah and Lily were Gus's family. Brandon wasn't prepared for this conversation. Especially when it involved a feisty teenage girl and her standoffish, breathtaking mother. "Would you like me to step out?"

Lily ignored him. "I had a great day and that sucks!"

Brandon, Gus, and Sarah glanced at each other, confused. "I don't understand why you are so upset, honey, if you had a good day?" Sarah sounded perplexed.

"Of course you wouldn't, Mom. You're too old and not a guy, so you wouldn't understand," Lily snapped as she stormed toward the door.

I'm a guy and I don't understand. Brandon thought silently.

"Wait." Sarah jumped from her seat, wincing from the quick movement and Brandon was right there, extending his hands.

Her cheeks, a light pink, drew Brandon in even more. "Thank you," Sarah whispered.

"Get back here, Lily," Sarah yelled as she teetered away.

Brandon hadn't expected her to comply, but Lily returned with a pool of tears threatening to spill over. Tears! Brandon didn't do tears—his own or girls'.

Sarah embraced her daughter. "What happened today, honey?"

Through her uncontrollable sobbing, Lily stammered out, "Oh, it was awful. Everyone liked me."

Gus chuckled behind them, and Brandon covered his laugh with a cough. Sarah pulled Lily off her shoulder, "I don't get it, Lily. Why is that a bad thing?"

"Mom, we should be home, our real home, with Dad. Do you think he's upset?" Lily rested her head back on Sarah's shoulder.

Embracing her daughter again, "Oh, honey, Dad would be thrilled that you are happy. He would want you to enjoy life wherever you are. I am elated that you had a great day."

"Mom, a boy offered to carry my books to class and I let him." She paused for a couple of seconds.

"I'm happy to rough him up if that will stop the tears." Brandon offered with a straight face, though he was teasing. Kinda.

"No." Lily giggled. "He is really cute, too. I love his bleach blonde hair and blue eyes. He looks like a surfer from back home, but no guy back home was this nice." Wiping her eyes, Lily straightened. "His name is Kurt Anderson. He goes to Grandpa's church, and he knew who I was because Grandpa asked for traveling mercies. He asked if I would sit with him at church this Sunday, so I'm thinking maybe I'll go with you this week."

"I'm sorry for being snappy." Lily apologized to Brandon.

He waved it off like it wasn't a big deal. "For what it's worth, Kurt is a solid kid."

Lily's smile filled her face and her eyes perked up. "How do you know Kurt?"

Maybe he could be good at this family thing. "I'm the teen's Sunday School teacher. I've known him for years, but it's been the last three that have shown me his true character."

Bolting from her seat, Lily clutched Brandon's forearms while she jumped up and down. "So, he's a nice guy, for real?"

"Yeah," Brandon chuckled, but stopped short when Sarah scowled at him. His stomach tightened. He changed Lily's tears into the dramatic teenage girl jumping he'd seen from the teens at church. Shouldn't Sarah be happy?

Gus interjected, "Honey, will you start dinner, please? I'm starving."

"Sure, Dad. Come on, Lily, you can help me." Sarah refused to even acknowledge Brandon.

"Ok." She acknowledged her mother. "Thank you, Brandon. Maybe you'll tell me more about him sometime."

Before Brandon could answer, Sarah linked her arm through Lily's. "I need some help to get inside."

Once the door slammed, Gus smacked Brandon on the shoulder.

"What are you doing?" Gus scolded Brandon. "Why are you making this so difficult?"

"Excuse me?"

Gus paused. "I'm not exactly sure, but you ticked Sarah off."

"I figured, but I don't know what I did. Maybe you should stop your matchmaking and you wouldn't be so upset."

Gus looked surprised that Brandon knew what he was trying to do. "You guys are perfect for each other. Trust me."

"You're coming to dinner to fix this."

"I'm wasting daylight and I won't push myself on someone who's made it clear that I'm not wanted."

Torn between reason and desire, Brandon's heart ached with the conflict. He'd found her at last, a woman who sparked something deep inside him, but her emotional distance was a wall he couldn't seem to break through.

CHAPTER 8

SARAH OPENED THE DOOR Friday morning to the unexpected sight of Jill; the smell of fresh coffee hung in the air.

She handed Sarah the to-go mug and insisted they go to breakfast at Hannigan's, the local general store. Feeling obligated, a sense of politeness overriding her better judgment, Sarah agreed to go.

With her life in turmoil and still unable to run, maybe clearing the air with Jill would ease her troubles.

Emily Hannigan, the owner of the bustling store, forced a smile when Sarah and Jill walked through the door. Emily's embrace was so strong that Sarah felt her own bones might break, her ribs compressed like twigs under the immense pressure. "I'm so sorry for your loss."

Tears welled in Sarah's eyes, not only for herself, but for Emily. She'd run this store by herself after her husband, Bill, and daughter, Autumn, died nineteen years ago. Bill rescued Emily from their burning house and went back in to save Autumn, but neither of them came out. The house collapsed, killing them both.

Sarah wasn't close with Autumn, because she was a star track athlete and Sarah's circle consisted of basketball players. Emily only closed the store for a week—long enough to bury her family. As a teenager, Sarah thought Emily was heartless. Now that Sarah had experienced the death of a spouse and parent, she understood why Emily had to return to work so fast.

"Thank you." She'd never wish the taunting memories on anyone. The nagging 'what if' questions were worse.

Emily brought coffee and took their order. "It won't be long. You gals came at a slow time."

Taking a sip of coffee, Jill commented, "I'm glad you're going to church. If we can just get Lily to go, she'll meet a lot of teens."

"Brandon convinced her to come."

"Hm. That's interesting."

"Not really. She met a boy at school and he's in Brandon's teen class, so she wants to go to church. God's the best matchmaker around. I'm not suggesting they get married or anything, but God's using the power of a crush to get Lily into church. I'll take it."

"Speaking of matchmakers, beware of Miss Clancy. She has a way about her. She can get anyone to share their deepest thoughts."

The bitterness and anger camping out in Sarah's heart anticipated Jill's interference.

"I'm not ready to share anything with anyone anytime soon." She didn't sound ungrateful for Jill's company, did she?

Emily dropped off their breakfast sandwiches and refilled their coffee mugs.

"I heard Brandon is renovating your house," Jill stated, but Sarah knew she was phishing for more.

"My dad's house."

Jill brushed her napkin over the corner of her lips. "Are there any sparks between you, too?"

"If by sparks you mean, I'm angrier than usual around him, then, yes."

Jill studied Sarah. "You're making me self-conscious."

"I'm very sorry for the way I treated you." Jill's tender voice, filled with sincerity. "I thought your relationship with Jerry was more than... It doesn't matter. I was insecure and I'm sorry."

"It's water under the bridge, but I must admit you drove me crazy. I couldn't get away fast enough. Your apology means a lot. Thank you."

"I have something important to tell you, but I'm worried you'll be angry with me again," Jill said, her voice trembled slightly.

Sarah blew out a breath. "I can't promise anything, but go for it."

"Jake was amazing and I'm so sorry you lost him early in our human minds, but don't miss God's plans for you. He left you behind to live."

What the heck? Sarah opened her mouth multiple times to retort, but nothing came out.

"I'm not saying you have to marry Brandon. Emotions aren't simple. I just want you to keep your eyes and heart open to be happy again."

The audacity. "Are you working with my dad? He had Brandon stay for dinner last night, even though he knew I was mad that Brandon swooped in and healed Lily's bad day."

"I'm only looking out for you. Gus said Lily was giving you a hard time about moving. Why were you upset that Brandon helped?"

"Jake's one-year anniversary is almost here. My purpose for living is to raise Lily."

"Your purpose is to do God's will and I think He has more in store for you than just raising Lily. Besides, Jake would want you to be happy."

How dare Jill use the same words Sarah had used on Lily yesterday! Why had she expected them to comfort Lily when they did very little for her?

The girls finished their breakfast with casual conversation about church, but Sarah's mind raced, not fully concentrating. How could Jill or her dad know what she needed when Sarah didn't?

As Sarah drove home, she felt peace wash over her where Jill was concerned, but her mind reeled between memories of Jake and the pull she was feeling toward Brandon.

Why would God put a genuine and good looking man in her life right now?

"Please give me answers," she pleaded to her Father in Heaven.

Pulling in the driveway next to Brandon's truck, a nervous energy filled her stomach. No. Maybe the egg on her sandwich had spoiled, causing her the fluttering feeling in her belly. Doubtful.

Maybe she couldn't run, but she could walk now that her knee felt more like itself.

"Dad, I'm going for a walk. Do you need anything before I go?" Sarah hollered when she entered the store.

Instead of greeting her dad, she crashed into Brandon. The strength of his strong arms caught her before she fell backwards.

Sarah immediately noticed Brandon's tanned and toned chest, the muscles rippling beneath his skin. Embarrassed, she quickly averted her gaze, the heat rising in her cheeks. She couldn't deny the images of his strong, muscular physique that flooded her mind, images she desperately tried to ignore. Then...

"Hi." His husky voice rendered her speechless.

CHAPTER 9

BRANDON DIDN'T BELIEVE IN love at first sight. But what about love at first touch? Definitely. When he carried Sarah home, his nerves were firing, but he attributed that to adrenaline from his run.

Now, his body reacted violently; his chest burned, and jolts shot through his abdomen when he wrapped his arms around her.

He shouldn't be holding this beautiful woman in his arms and staring into her eyes, but he couldn't stop himself, either. He'd release her if she moved or squirmed away. She didn't. Her fingers gripped his shoulders. Interesting. Maybe her perfectly constructed walls were crumbling.

Eventually, he steadied her. Their lingering touch warmed his core. "Are you okay?"

"Yeah. Sorry. I'm looking for my dad. Have you seen him?"

Disappointment grumbled in his gut. If only she'd been looking for him, he could pull her closer and kiss her lips. Since he carried her home, kissing her consumed his thoughts during the day and his dreams at night.

"Uh. Yeah," Brandon ran his fingers through his hair. "He said he'd be right back."

Sarah covered her twitching lips with her hand. "What's so funny?" Brandon questioned, hoping he didn't regret asking.

"You left a trail of sawdust behind." Sarah gestured to Brandon's hair.

"That's funny to you?" His lips tugged at the corners. "If you think that's funny, you'll love this," Brandon teased, shaking his hair and shirt in her direction.

Sarah shrieked, "Stop that." She put her hands up to cover her face.

"I'm sorry, Sarah. I can't tell if you're serious when you laugh." Her sweet sounds tugged at Brandon's heartstrings.

Agility was her friend. She took a big side leap, enticing him with her movement. The way her fitted shirt and leggings accentuated her features had already captured his attention.

Brandon filled her space. "Let me help." Toe to toe, he wiped the sawdust off her shoulder and head.

"It's in my hair?" She asked, the pitch of her tone increased. But the teasing glint in her eyes and the subtle twitch of her lips, trying to hold back a laugh, pushed Brandon even closer.

"You're pretty. Sawdust and all." Brandon hung his head. "That was bad. For the record, it sounded much better in my head."

"You should have left it there," she teased.

"Ouch. You're brutal," Brandon said, dragging his fingers up her arm.

Brandon searched Sarah's eyes. If she attempted to move, Brandon would let her go. Since that wasn't the case, he dragged his fingers through her hair. "Just making sure I got all the sawdust." His voice, low and husky, surprised him.

Again, this woman had him doing and saying things he wouldn't normally do. Flashes of Superman and Kryptonite along with Samson and Delilah careened through his mind. Strong men who had a deadly pull toward their desires. The thought vanished as rapidly as it appeared.

He never said he could flirt, but fortunately, Sarah played along. "Oh, really? I guess you are the gentleman people say you are."

Had she been asking about him? That thought had his heart doing a happy dance. Her full lips had been calling him for days.

"Sarah." He brushed the hair away from her face. Of all the places he imagined kissing her, Gus's store wasn't one of them. Wood particles hadn't covered him head to toe either, but who was he to rob God of His good works? Brandon leaned in for a taste.

"Ahem."

They froze at the sound of her father. Then Sarah took a big step back and cut off their eye contact.

"Am I interrupting something?" Gus asked with a smirk.

Eager to act on his thoughts, Brandon opened his mouth to tell Gus the interruption would set construction back a day. He preferred to take Sarah out and reunite her with the area.

Instead, she spoke first. "Nothing of interest, Dad, so you can wipe that look off your face."

"What look?" he played dumb.

Sarah silently questioned him with raised eyebrows. Surprisingly, Gus didn't crumble. Brandon found the look intimidating.

"I was looking for you and ran into Brandon; nothing more."

Her words left a bitter taste in his mouth, swallowing his great idea.

"I'm glad I found you, Sarah. I left a couple of messages for you on the counter regarding jobs, and I wanted to let you know Brandon is staying for dinner tonight."

Sarah questioned, "He is?" Simultaneously, Brandon remarked. "I am?"

He couldn't stay for dinner again. Brandon never burdened anyone; especially someone he cared about. Is that how he felt? His body expressed something far deeper than mere care. His pulse raced and his slick hands would make gripping his tools a challenge. The hammering in his chest and rapid breathing revealed something powerful. Obviously, not love. He hadn't known her long enough, right?

His previous relationships were more like consecutive dates without depth. The women held back, waiting to hear his thoughts, then just agreed with him. They also didn't appreciate his devotion to the family business.

"Oh, no. you're not having Sarah cook for me, again." Gus's attempt earlier in the week to bring his daughter and him together hadn't gone well.

Gus pushed his shoulders back. "Who said she was cooking? Lily wants burgers, but that's not Sarah's speciality; it's yours. I figured you'd grill for us before we have to cover it for the season."

Brandon snuck a look at Sarah. She pressed her lips together. Groaning, he conceded. "Okay. I'll stay if I'm wanted."

Sarah's eyes darted between the men. "What?" she asked, feigning ignorance.

"You know." Gus barked. "You'll behave at dinner this time?"

She glared at her dad. "Uh."

Brandon spoke before she could respond. "I don't recall anything she needs to apologize for."

Sure, the grape juice stain is still on his jeans from where she *acciden-tally* spilled it, but he'd turn them into work jeans. No problem.

"Oh, come on." Gus scoffed. "My daughter has better manners than she showed. We all know she's grieving, but so is Lily, so am I. You don't see us giving people the cold shoulder."

"Ha. If it's my cold shoulder that bothered you, then maybe I should yell and tell people exactly what I think like Lily does…"

Yes. Please. Maybe. Only if it won't hurt too bad. Brandon's mind wandered.

"…or maybe I should try matchmaking like you, Dad." Sarah folded her arms across her chest, challenging him to deny his works.

With a curt nod, he said, "Now, you're talking. Start by matching up with this guy and you'll be on track."

She threw her hands in the air before she stormed away, muttering, "Good grief."

The door slammed, and Gus turned to Brandon. "What are you doing?"

What did he want to hear? That I was trying to kiss his daughter. Or that I made a fool of myself by teasing her.

"Treating her like a child won't get you anywhere. I helped you."

Gus nodded. "You're right, but—"

"Stop trying to set us up. If it's God's will, no one can change it."

"Yeah, yeah. Get to work." Gus ordered, shooing Brandon away.

On his way to his truck, Brandon had the feeling someone was watching him. He looked over his shoulder toward the house, and the door's curtain swayed. The idea of Sarah watching him had his heart racing.

He wanted her to give him a chance, but could he convince her, or was he destined to stay married to his business?

CHAPTER 10

SARAH WOKE TO HER phone vibrating on the nightstand. Despite her better judgment, Sarah rolled onto her stomach and answered the call. "Hi, Jill, it's quite early, don't ya think?"

"Yes, maybe, but I was hoping we could go shopping this morning and then meet for an early movie tonight and I didn't want you to make any other plans," Jill explained.

Going shopping didn't appeal to Sarah. First of all she didn't have a job, so all the money she saved before moving was going toward Lily right now. Furthermore, Sarah was never a shopping girl. She liked to either buy it online or go to the store, get it, and leave. Saying no to Jill wasn't easy because she pestered people until she got what she wanted. A strong feeling within, answered for Sarah. "Sure. I'd love to catch a movie, but shopping?" Sarah questioned.

Jill pestered until Sarah agreed to both! "Great. I'll be over about eight to pick you up. Then I'll drop you back off in time to see Lily. We'll meet at the theater for the six o'clock," Jill explained.

The ladies quickly said their goodbyes then Sarah hurried around the house like Lily trying to get ready. Sarah and Lily split a bagel with peanut butter, before Lily hopped on the bus.

Gus seemed overly excited about his daughter's plans, but she dismissed the nagging thought when Jill arrived. Sarah hopped into the woman's convertible BMW. "This is a beautiful car. I bet it's great in the summer. Maine still has summer, right?" Sarah teased.

"You really miss Florida, huh?" Jill asked with a sigh.

"I miss the weather. I hate running in the cold, it bothers my lungs," Sarah explained.

"From what I've heard you should be pretty warm while you're running." Jill joked. "Remember you live in a small town again. People see you running with Brandon every morning, what's going on there?"

"Nothing." Sarah said defensively. "I'm only walking right now because of my knee, and he meets up with me. I'm not going to be rude." Sarah stopped explaining herself. "People should mind their own business!"

"Settle down," Jill urged. I think you and Brandon are great for each other. What's the problem?"

Sarah stared out the side window, unsure of how much to reveal to Jill. She wasn't sure if she could truly trust her. Jake's motto was always, *Trust no one*. "I'm a widow," she stated bluntly.

"And..." Jill waited for something else as if that wasn't enough explanation. When Sarah remained quiet Jill said, pointing a finger in the air, "Know what I think? You like Brandon and you're afraid to admit it because you think you should be all alone now that Jake is gone."

Sarah studied her. How could Jill know her thoughts?

"Look Sarah, you are beautiful and young. Men are going to be interested in you. The question is whether you are going to live life or just ride through until it's your time to go. What does God want you to do?" Jill pushed.

"I don't know, He didn't tell me," Sarah replied. "Besides, Brandon is focused on building his business. He doesn't have time to deal with a woman who doesn't know what she wants."

"Did you ask?" Jill inquired. "Look," Jill continued when Sarah didn't respond, "I hope you know that I just want you to be happy. Think about what I said. Maybe you should talk to Pastor Pete. He's good with these kinds of situations. For now, let's shop."

Jill pulled into a parking spot right outside her favorite department store, shut the car off, and gave Sarah's hand a reassuring squeeze. "You'll see; everything will work out because the Bible tells us to knock and doors will open."

Sarah wasn't knocking though. Why did Jill and her dad think she needed to move on?

After the ladies shopping trip, Jill dropped Sarah off at home just as Lily stepped off the bus. "See you at six," Jill yelled before Sarah shut the car door.

Sarah nodded in agreement and waved bye to Jill.

"Hey Mom, how was your day?" Lily asked with a smile.

Relieved to see that Brandon was gone, Sarah wrapped her arm around Lily's shoulder. "Jill and I went shopping and I bought you a new outfit."

"Great, can I see it?" Lily reached for the bag.

"Here you go honey, I hope you like it." Lily opened the bag and pulled out a gray sweater with a big scoop neck and a pair of black jeans.

"Mom, it's great. Thank you. What's for dinner?"

"I'm going to ask Grandpa to order take out because I'm going to a movie with Jill," Sarah replied. "Is that okay, or do you need me here tonight?"

Lily laughed out loud. "Mom, go have fun. I'll be fine with Grandpa. He raised you. I think he'll be able to take good care of me."

Too bad. Sarah didn't want to go anywhere, but she already promised. "Hey, how did you like the coach?"

"He made us run five fire drills because some girls weren't paying attention." When Sarah looked at her with a confused look, she explained that her coach refused to call them suicides, so he called them fire drills. Sarah recalled one horrible practice having to run for consequences. She threw up all over the gym. Jake helped her clean up and drove her home. Then he drove Gus back to the school to get Sarah's car. *I miss you, Jake.*

"Sarah!" Gus's voice brought her back to the present. "You're still going out with Jill, right?"

That was odd. How did her dad know her plans? She hadn't told him.

Before she could answer, Lily did. "Yes, she's going to change right now." Lily turned Sarah around, facing the stairs and gave her a little shove. It was a quick glance, but Sarah noticed the suspicious look between her dad and daughter.

When Sarah arrived at the theater, she waited in the lobby for Jill, but with five minutes until showtime she called Jill to make sure everything was okay.

"Sarah, please don't be mad at me. It was all your dad's idea."

Before she progressed Jill's words, Sarah turned around, confused and frustrated. There stood Brandon. "You should have told me, Jill," Sarah replied. "I'll talk to you later."

Sarah put her phone in her pocket and looked up at Brandon, "So were you in on the plan, or an innocent bystander?"

Placing his hands in his pocket, Brandon rocked on his heels and smiled staring directly in Sarah's eyes. "I mentioned to your dad about the movie. It wasn't my idea to trick you. I planned on asking you, but your dad said... It doesn't matter. We don't have to stay if you don't want to."

With his navy blue polo and what appeared to be new dark blue jeans, he momentarily took her breath away. The way he offered to forget about the movie told her there was something more to him than just his good looks.

Sarah thought about it for a moment and decided that she really wanted to see the new movie with Sylvester Stallone and Arnold Schwarzenegger. "We're already here, no point in leaving." Brandon opened the door for Sarah and placed his hand on her lower back, guiding her into the theater.

Sarah enjoyed the movie, but she felt Brandon gazing at her throughout the whole thing and it made her feel self-conscious and special at the same time.

Walking across the parking lot, Sarah challenged, "Race ya?"

Bending over laughing Brandon replied, "You're on! But don't cry when you lo-."

Before Brandon could finish, Sarah jumped the gun, "Go!" She took off in a flash.

Running to catch up, "You cheated," Brandon yelled. As he approached, Sarah pushed harder and her knee buckled. Down she went—again.

"Are you okay? Here let me carry you the rest of the way."

Sarah rejected the idea. "I'm fine. Can you just help me up, please?"

Brandon ignored her rejection. He scooped her up and carried her to his truck. "You'll have to pick your car up tomorrow; you can't drive," Brandon insisted. "I'll go let the theater manager know what happened," he added.

The whole way home Brandon and Sarah found something to talk about. Brandon informed Sarah that she needed the doctor to check out her knee again and maybe she should rethink running for a while. While Sarah appreciated his concern, she always completed things she committed to.

"So, how did you acquire such a booming business," Sarah changed the subject.

"My dad handed it down to me, but I worked with him since my sixteenth birthday, officially. Before that, I learned what hard labor meant. When I started getting paid, things seemed easier," Brandon explained.

"That's a great way to start out your career; already successful," Sarah sounded impressed.

"Maybe you could pass that on to my dad." Brandon jokingly suggested, though the idea actually seemed pretty good. She didn't like the way his dad put him down all the time. "My dad expected me to expand the business by now with a whole crew." He paused. "I think he's disappointed because I haven't," Brandon added.

At a loss for words, Sarah looked at Brandon with sympathetic eyes, "I'm sorry. Does he argue with you about this or does he let you run the business the way you want?" Sarah quickly asked to keep the conversation going.

"I avoid talking about the business at all cost, but he can nag better than any woman ever thought of!" Brandon laughed to lighten the mood and then he leaned over and gently pushed Sarah's shoulder emphasizing his comment.

"Yeah, Yeah, that's why you're single right? You don't want to be nagged." Sarah shocked herself with her comment. She didn't want to lead him on or encourage relationship talk; the words just came out of her mouth without even thinking.

"The right woman could nag me and that would be perfectly fine." Brandon winked at Sarah.

Did he mean she could nag him? Certainly not. They didn't know each other well enough.

Brandon pulled in the driveway, put the truck in park, and turned off the engine. "We're here. Stay put, Sarah, and I'll come get you." Brandon flashed Sarah a quick smile and exited the truck.

Feeling self-conscious, Sarah's body stiffen. Sarah was happy for her years of fall cheerleading. She quickly recalled, *it's always easier to lift someone when their limbs are locked.* She only hoped that the same theory applied in this type of position.

As Brandon opened the door he put one arm under Sarah's knees and instructed her to put her arm around his shoulder. All Sarah could think about was how broad shouldered and strong Brandon felt. This was different from Jake's build and Sarah couldn't help but notice that she liked it. Her limbs relaxed, as if she were comfortable in his arms. That wasn't the case, right?

Sarah's heart ached when he placed her feet down on the farmer's porch. Instantly, she missed the warmth from his chest.

I should not be thinking of him like this. Sarah thought silently to herself. *What would Jake think? Am I betraying him?* Sarah shook her head in a way to remove these thoughts and looked up at Brandon. "Thank you so much for saving me...again. You really are a good guy, huh?"

Smiling and staring directly into Sarah's eyes, Brandon picked her up again and placed her on the porch bench swing then he sat next to her and softly replied, "You tell me. Have I convinced you yet?" He rested his hand on her thigh.

Her heart pounded out of control. "Brandon, you can't be saying things like that. It is too hard for me right now. I'm doing my best to live like Pastor Pete tells me and my thoughts are my worst enemy. Plus, I have Lily to focus on and I have to help my dad."

"Sometimes you let your guard down, Sarah, and we have fun together. I know you feel something. Other times, like now, you guard your heart or your mind," Brandon sounded defeated. "I will pray tonight that you do one thing—stop hiding behind your responsibilities. Lily is doing just fine. You have not faulted in your role as a mother, and your dad takes care of himself just fine. You know he does not need your help; he just wanted you home."

Sarah stood up forcing all her weight on one leg, "You can pray all you want, but the fact remains that I do have family responsibilities and I will not put them on the back burner, so I can pursue some romantic relationship with anyone, no matter how attractive and sweet he may be." Sarah winced as she realized that she said that last part out loud. Judging by the smile on Brandon's face she knew she couldn't take anything back.

Brandon stood up and held Sarah's arm, "I'm going to leave. I'm sorry I upset you. Brandon spontaneously kissed Sarah gently on the cheek. Do you need help getting into the house?"

"No, I'll hobble inside. I'm used to it now. Thank you though for a great movie and for getting me home. I really do appreciate it," Sarah assured him. She limped to the door where Gus greeted her and helped her the rest of the way in the house.

"How was your evening with Brandon?" Gus asked in a chipper voice.

Glaring at her dad she said, "Very funny. You set this all up. Stop interfering in my life." Sarah demanded.

"I thought you needed a night out with a good guy," Gus replied as he helped Sarah to the couch.

"Dad, life is way too hard. I certainly don't need you meddling in my life making it more difficult for me. I feel too old to be feeling like a young teenager in love. I feel too young to be a widow and I feel guilty for my feelings," Sarah finally confessed.

"Oh, Sarah, let's talk."

Sarah shook her head and used the arm of the couch to hoist herself up. "No, I'm tired dad. Please don't make plans for me in the future," Sarah requested.

Sarah hobbled upstairs hoping a good night rest would heal her body.

When she cleaned out her pockets, Sarah saw the movie ticket stub and threw it in her wastebasket. Suddenly, she decided to keep it, though not sure why. Taking it from the trash, she placed it on her bureau. She enjoyed the carefree spirit she had felt tonight. Would she be able to forget this night? Did she want to?

CHAPTER 11

SARAH HADN'T TALKED TO Brandon since they went to the movie. Why would he tell her he liked her? And the kiss he gave her on the cheek, what was that?

For three days, Sarah purposely woke early and left right after Lily, before Brandon arrived. She didn't know what to say to him and she didn't want to lead him on. She also made plans to be busy during dinner. Sarah couldn't see herself dating anyone—ever again.

One afternoon, she ran out of places to go, so she traveled to her favorite spot as a teenager when she wanted to be alone—the Cove. She watched the waves roll in and out and thought about Jake. She constantly wondered if Jake was disappointed in her for allowing her mind to drift to another man. Sarah couldn't deny Brandon's great looks and if that was all, she'd be able to avoid him, but Sarah finally admitted to herself that he was a really nice guy, too.

Sarah felt all alone. She wanted someone to tell her what she should think and feel. Instead she picked up rocks and started skimming them across the water. Normally, she talked to her mom about these kinds of things, and this thought made Sarah more sad.

Without anyone to share this with, Sarah did the only thing she could think of—she sat in the sand and started praying. *God, I know I haven't really relied on you in a long time and I am sorry for that, but I need you to tell me what to do.*

That was all Sarah could manage before she noticed Pastor Pete and his wife, Pearle, walking hand in hand along the water's edge. The couple strolled over to Sarah. Pearle never let go of her grip on her husband as she greeted Sarah with a smile and slight wave with her free hand. "Hi, Sarah. Are you adjusting to Maine weather?"

Sarah lifted her head, zipped up her second fleece jacket, and used her hand as a sun visor over her eyes, "Not yet. Wearing pants and a fleece in October is quite foreign to me. Actually, I'm hoping to return to Florida soon for a job. Well, I don't know what's going on with anything right now, so I'm just going through the motions." Sarah dropped her hand and started to doodle with her pointer finger in the sand. "Please don't say anything about Florida; no one knows yet," Sarah surprised herself. Why did she tell them?

Pastor Pete knelt on one knee and rested his hand on Sarah's shoulder, "Do you want to talk, Sarah?"

Pearle urged, "I can go look for shells—something Pete hates to do."

Sarah paused a while contemplating the offer. Finally, she spoke, "If you don't mind, I have a lot going on and I just don't know how to handle it all."

With a hop in her step, Pearle turned around, "I'll be back in a while."

Pastor sat down in the sand. "Before you start, let me pray." He took Sarah's hand, "God, thank you for this opportunity to talk with Sarah. I know some would call it a coincidence that we were on the same beach today, but I know this was a divine appointment. I ask that you help Sarah formulate her thoughts, so she can express them to me and hopefully Sarah will hear Your will for her in our conversation. Lord, I ask that I hear You, so I can help lead her the way You direct. Please, Lord, help Sarah find the peace she needs in her life, amen."

Sarah pulled her hand from Pastor Pete's. "Thank you." Sarah started doodling in the sand with her finger and digging her bare feet into the sand. She still felt a little uncomfortable talking to Pastor Pete, since she had only known him for about two months and because he wasn't much older than she was. Somehow though Sarah found the words. "Lily didn't want to come to Maine, but now that she's met Kurt, and made the varsity basketball team, she is happy to be here. I can't take these things from her by moving back. She'll definitely think I'm trying to ruin her life... again." Sarah erased the picture she made in the sand with her palm.

Pastor Pete laughed and rested his arms on his knees. "I'm sure you're doing what you think is best for the both of you."

"See, I hate the cold weather, so when it started getting cold, I applied for a teaching position in Florida that I found online. I should hear after Thanksgiving break whether or not they want to hire me. I don't even know if I want to go back... I just don't know what I want. That's the problem."

"Is cold weather the only reason you want to return to Florida?"

"Not exactly," Sarah replied as she dropped her head looking at the sand. "I am having a hard time being around Brandon Taylor. He's always at my dad's house fixing something and Dad invites him to stay for dinner every night. I don't mind the extra dish to prepare, but it seems as though everyone is trying to set us up. My dad and Lily purposely leave us alone when they go to get pizza or what not. He's a nice enough guy, but I'm a widow, I can't date another man. I have to focus on Lily now," Sarah explained.

Tipping his head back and opening his mouth, "Awe, I get it now. Your husband dies, so your life must die, romantically speaking, too."

Finally, someone got it! Sarah nodded her head in agreement, but before she could say anything, Pastor continued. "You do know that when a person's spouse dies, God allows that person to remarry right? God wants you to obey Him, which means you need to follow Him and do as He asks you. Do you think He's asking you to return to Florida, or is that you?"

Sarah ran her hand through her long blonde hair that started blowing every which way with a huge wind gust. "It's probably me. I don't have a great sense that I should go, even if they offered it to me."

His eyebrows raised as he shrugged and nodded.

"Okay, so Florida is out. One problem down, one to go."

"Nice try. I led you to your own answer about Florida, but this one is not going to be so easy. You need to read God's word everyday and pray in order to hear what God has in store for you. Maybe it is Brandon, which I must say wouldn't be the worst thing in the world." Pastor Pete leaned forward in an effort to get Sarah to make eye contact with him.

"I know he's a nice guy."

Before she could say any more, Pastor interrupted her to let her know that Brandon is very interested in her.

Sarah's head shot up in the Pastor's direction, "How do you know this?"

Pastor Pete smiled at Sarah. "I have my ways," he joked with her. "It's written all over his face. The way he admires you during service makes his feelings clear. I remember people telling me that's how I looked at Pearle and I know how much I love her, so I can just imagine what Brandon is thinking."

Pastor's back straightened, "Maybe God just wants you to be open to possibilities. You need to listen to Him and do as He says, not what you want."

Sarah spotted Pearle with two hands full of shells.

"Thank you Pastor for your wisdom. You've really just given me more to think about." Sarah felt discouraged and hopeful at the same time.

Pastor Pete stood up to greet Pearle and extended his hands to help her carry the shells. "Anytime, Sarah, you know where my office is; come and see me. Let me leave you with this verse from the Book of Jeremiah to pray about. *I know the plans I have for you,* declares the Lord, *plans to prosper you and not to harm you, plans to give you hope and a future.*"

Sarah watched the happy couple walk back down the beach and then she turned her attention back on the ocean. Sarah sat a long while in silence staring at the ocean.

"Jake, I love you, but I have to let you go."

CHAPTER 12

"I REALLY NEED YOUR help here." Gus pleaded to his daughter on the phone. "I'm far behind on setting up the store and Brandon needs some help too."

Brandon cringed, hoping Sarah wouldn't keep avoiding him.

"That's fine honey," replied Gus. "We'll keep busy until you come out. Thanks dear, you're a lifesaver."

"What'd she say?" Brandon's eagerness getting the best of him.

"She'll be out soon."

Twenty minutes later, Sarah entered the store looking pretty as ever. Her hair flowing down her back. The black leggings clung to her toned legs and she swam in the University of Florida sweatshirt.

Sarah made eye contact with him when she entered and it warmed his heart. They hadn't spoken in days and he missed her.

"Sarah, honey. I'm so glad you're here. This large harvest is taking all my time.," Gus began.

"Can you help me finish winterizing the greenhouse?" Brandon asked, his eagerness showing. "I need someone small to fix the storage place at the top,"

"Sure."

"Thanks, honey. I'll be back here if you guys need me."

As they walked toward the greenhouse, he felt like a teenager around the girl he liked. Fortunately, she started a conversation.

"By the way, I'm really sorry for being so snappy the other day. Thank you for taking such good care of me and helping my dad get my car from the theater," Sarah said as she put her hair up in a ponytail, showing off her long neck.

"No problem." He dismissed her comment. "Are you ready for this?" She nodded.

Brandon held the ladder while Sarah climbed to the top of the greenhouse. "Did I forget to mention that I am not a fan of heights."

It took every ounce of self-control he possessed, but he kept his eyes focused on her feet as she pulled herself up one rung at a time.

Laughing at Sarah, "Don't worry, I'll protect you. I'm getting pretty good at it," Brandon joked.

"Yeah, sorry about that." She said, pulling the plastic tight and using the staple gun to secure it in place.

"Nothing to be sorry about. I'm glad I was there to help you."

If she'd let him be there for her all the time, he'd be even happier. Regardless of what his dad said, he could have a successful business and a serious girlfriend. What made Caleb think he could have a wife and the business, yet his son couldn't? Brandon's workload doubled in the last couple of weeks, booking him up until at least February. He would have both.

Sarah finished and announced, "I'm on my way down. Hold the ladder please." Sarah reached the ground safely and turned to Brandon, "Is there anything else you need?" Sarah wiped the dirt off her tights and used the back of her hand to fling a strand of hair out of her eyes.

"Thank you so much for your help." Brandon replied. "The greenhouse is winterized and ready for your dad to start planting. This is earlier than last year, so he might have an even better season next year."

"I don't know about that. I only saw the last harvest, but it seemed fruitful," Sarah said with a nervous laugh. "I'll be swapping out the old cash register Dad used if you need anything else."

Sarah began to walk away when Brandon called out to her. "I had a great time at the movies. I'm sorry about what I said..."

Turning around Sarah half smiled. "You should never apologize for saying things people need to hear."

"Maybe we can do it again sometime?"

Her smile grew. "Maybe."

Sarah left Brandon in the store alone, so he turned to his Father above.

"Lord, I need your help. How many times am I going to put myself out there?" Brandon suddenly thought of the passage where Jesus tells people to forgive their neighbor seventy times seven times. Maybe the same applies when trying to help people see something they can't. Why can't Sarah see that she is more than a widow? She deserves to be happy again. "I trust that you've got this Lord, please give me the strength I need to get through this trying situation in my life. Give me peace, amen."

CHAPTER 13

AFTER SPENDING THE DAY on the phone with the company in charge of renting out her house in Florida and getting directions for her Maine teaching certificate, Sarah needed a break.

This week, Lily masked her pain by surrounding herself with kids she'd met at school. Surely, Kurt was at the top of the list. At home, her outbursts were less and her tone less harsh, but still present.

Sarah buried her grief. Her headphones and running shoes called her name. Though her knee felt better, Sarah walked the lonely road, only kept company by her thoughts.

She could no longer deny the magnetic pull of Brandon Taylor, his presence eclipsing everything else, making her forget the boundaries she'd set.

She and Jake never talked about what would happen when God called one of them home. Who expects to lose a husband in his thirties? Not Sarah.

"God, please." Sarah didn't know how to finish. Please send Brandon away. Please help ease the pain. Please give answers. Maybe all three?

A wave of emptiness washed over her as thoughts of her past life ran through her mind. Memories turned her bitter, fueling her adrenaline. Instinctively, her pace turned into speed walking, then a slow-paced run.

Jake's favorite sayings were, "Always forgive" and "Be happy." He didn't understand the pain and grief associated with losing a loved one. With his last breath, God stripped his hurt away, and now he basked in the glory of God.

For Sarah, guilt ate away at her every time she thought about Jake stopping at the store to get her flowers that day. If she hadn't told him she had a rough day with a student, he wouldn't have. Then he wouldn't have been at the intersection when a fire-red Camaro tried to outrun the police in Central Florida. When the driver bolted through a red light at one hundred miles per hour, he side-swiped Jake's small, aging hatchback and sent him to the hospital with life-threatening injuries. Sarah arrived at the hospital to see Jake, who held on to give her a message. She'll never forget it.

"I love you and Lily more than anything. Take care of her and live your best life. I'll always be with you." Like that, Jake was gone.

The problem was that he wasn't with her. Instead, God dangled another beautiful man in front of her like a piece of unforbidden fruit. Maybe that was only her perception. The very thought of Brandon initiated more guilt.

"Brandon, you're eating with us again?" Lily's tone wasn't rude, just curious.

Gus shook his head. "What is it with you gals? Can't you see a good man when he's standing right in front of you?"

Sarah froze, every muscle in her body tensed. As their gazes met, the hurt in Lily's eyes mirrored Sarah's.

"I didn't mean it the way you're thinking. I love Jake like a son. But I will not let you," he pointed at Sarah, "isolate and punish yourself for something God did. No one has control over when they die."

"What about suicide?" Lily questioned Gus's logic.

Gus pursed his lips. "No. God even controls that. If God doesn't want that person to die, He won't let it happen. Our lives are determined before we're born, so nothing surprises God. It's sad and I don't wish that type of pain on anyone—"

"What about you?" Sarah interrupted. "Mom's been gone a year and you're acting like nothing changed."

"Now, you wait a minute. I loved your mother very much. You haven't been around the last year, so you don't know how I grieved. The happiness you're seeing is because my daughter and granddaughter came back to me."

Sarah's shoulders rounded, and her head dropped. If she were being honest, having Brandon witness this embarrassed her. He probably felt out of place and that's why he moved toward the door. Moments later, she showed her face. Tears pooled in her eyes. "I'm sorry, Dad." Sarah stepped into her dad's embrace.

Lily wrapped her arms around both of them. "I love you guys."

"Give Brandon a chance to make you happy again," Gus whispered in Sarah's ear.

"You told me Dad would want me to be happy. Wouldn't he want that for you, too?" Lily asked.

"Stop ganging up on me," Sarah ordered, a playful glint in her eyes, a teasing smile playing on her lips.

She pulled away and retreated to the kitchen. Upon her return, she handed a plate of pressed burgers to Brandon. "Impress us with your grilling skills."

"No, can do." He replied, catching Sarah off guard. "Not without an assistant."

Sarah shrugged. "Dad, Brandon needs help."

"Someone under sixty—"

"No problem—"

Brandon rested his hand on her shoulder and fire seared through her shirt. "Before you tell Lily to help me. I'd like you to be my assistant."

"Aww!" Lily cooed.

"Traitor." Sarah growled at her daughter.

Lily put her hands on her hips. "Every girl desires a guy who wants her around."

I had one. Sarah shook her head free of those thoughts, trying to heed the advice of many about living life. Who would blame her if she moved on with a very attractive and kind man? No one.

While they grilled, Brandon told her all about his dream of going on a mission trip. Many times, her brain compared Brandon with Jake and she had to force the thoughts away.

"Would you like to hang out this weekend? We can do whatever you want." Brandon moved closer to her. The pull toward him, hotter than the fire coming from the grill.

"You might regret saying that." Sarah tugged on his shirt, leaning back so she could attempt to keep eye contact.

"Never. I'm enthralled with you, so as long as I'm with you, it doesn't matter what we do."

Brandon leaned in quickly and dropped a kiss on her cheek. Then he returned to the grill and flipped the burgers.

Sarah's insides were melting like the cheese Brandon placed on the burgers. She hadn't felt the new giddy feelings of a relationship since she met Jake in high school.

"If it's alright with you, I'd like to get your number before I leave tonight."

"What if I forget to give it to you?" Sarah's playful words hung in the air.

"Then I'll ask Gus for it." Brandon winked at her.

She shook her head and laughed. She really laughed, and her shoulders relaxed, feeling lighter every second she talked with this man.

Brandon gazed at her with liquid milk chocolate eyes, so kind and alluring.

Did she have the ability to start over? She hoped so.

CHAPTER 14

BRANDON BLINKED AND SEPTEMBER vanished. His favorite moments were chatting with Sarah at lunch time. Gus could never join them. Conveniently, he had "business to attend" in the house.

"Did you bring a change of clothes for this afternoon?" Sarah asked as she hopped up on the tailgate of his truck.

Yesterday, Sarah's doctor cleared her to run again. An overwhelming tightness ached in his chest until she promised she'd wait until he could go with her.

"I'm ready."

Sarah sighed. "Did you already run today? Running with me won't give you the same excursion as if you did it on your own."

"You qualified for the Boston Marathon," he said, choking on his laugh. "I'm hoping to keep up with you."

"You're being too kind."

Brandon still hadn't convinced Sarah to let him take her out, but he considered lunch together every day as dates.

"Question time." Brandon put his sandwich down on his lunch bag, rubbing his palms down his legs.

"Okay, but I'll start this time." Sarah looked toward the sky and then met his gaze. Whatever she saw caused her to stumble over her words. "W-where would you like to visit?"

"That's easy, Ireland. I'd trace my ancestors. A mission trip anywhere I'm called is high on my list, too."

"Of course, you'd have to upstage my answer."

"Shoot. Where'd you go?" Brandon picked up his sandwich and took a big bite, hoping Sarah wouldn't clam up on him like she sometimes did during their questions.

"The Mediterranean beaches and charming villages of Italy." She shrugged.

"Gorgeous. I'd take you there in a heartbeat."

For a split second, they froze, processing his words. "I was calling Italy gorgeous, not you." Sarah's eyes widened. "No. Wait." Brandon inhaled a breath. "Let me try that again. Sarah, you are stunning, period. Italy, equally wonderful, is a place I'd take you, if you let me." He let out another breath.

"Nice save."

"Thank you. But it was all the truth." The chilly air between them rose twenty degrees in the last few minutes. The thought of kissing Sarah filled him with equal parts of longing and dread. With each sunrise, he hoped that day would be perfect for a kiss. By sunset, dread weighed him down when it didn't happen. He couldn't rush her and risk scaring her away, so he'd have to pray harder tonight for more patience and self-control. God knows he needed both.

"My turn." Brandon shifted the conversation. "I can't believe we haven't asked this yet. Favorite movie."

"Easy. Wizard of Oz. You?" Sarah sipped her water.

"Rocky Series."

Sarah swung her legs. "I love Rocky IV."

"Maybe we could watch it together sometime." Brandon cringed. So much for not pressuring her. "I'm sorry. Sarah, I really like you and I want to spend time with you. I don't mean to annoy you—"

"Sure. I'd love to."

Brandon blinked. "Did you just agree to a date with me?"

"No." She smirked. "I agreed to watch a movie with you."

"What's the difference?" Brandon asked her to clarify.

She shrugged. "I'm not sure. It just doesn't sound as scary."

He understood what she meant, so he didn't tease her. Even if he didn't understand, he wouldn't have said anything, fearing she would change her mind.

"How about tonight after dinner?" Now he was being pushy, but again, he didn't want her to change her mind.

"Possibly. Right now, you need to get back to constructing that." Sarah pointed at the lean-to he started yesterday. She doesn't know it's for her car. Gus wanted to surprise her.

Brandon hopped off the truck and held out his hand for Sarah. She placed her soft fingers in his rough palm and a spark of electricity ran up his arm. The alarmed look on Sarah's face made him wonder if she felt it, too.

He pulled her down. She landed toe-to-toe with him. Every nerve cell in his body screamed, *kiss her*. He leaned down and kissed her forehead.

Her shoulders shivered, warming his insides even more. He appreciated the cool October temperature. Any hotter and he'd explode.

Brandon waved to Kurt and Lily and then helped Sarah into his truck after dinner.

As soon as Brandon latched his seat belt, Sarah asked, "You're sure Kurt is a good kid? I wouldn't have let Lily go anywhere with him, but you say he's a good kid and my dad trusts you... But I'm nervous."

"He's as good as they get. Don't worry." Brandon reassured her.

Sarah nodded. "He seemed respectable, but Jake warned I could be easily duped sometimes. Sorry."

"For what?"

"I don't mean to talk about Jake. I'm not trying to throw him in your face or anything. Not that we're dating or anything like that. It was just something my dad said to me."

Inwardly, Brandon chuckled. He didn't mind seeing Sarah stumble on her words, like he had earlier. If she was any like him, it happened because she was nervous around him. Not that Brandon wanted her to be uneasy in his presence, but it showed she wanted to impress him, and that gave him more hope.

"Jake is the father of your child, your high school sweetheart, the man you married. He helped make you who you are and I like what I see."

She blushed. Brandon waited weeks for this. Had he finally broken through her walls? *God, please say yes.*

"I forgot how quick the weather can shift. We've gone from warm days and semi-chilly nights to this unpleasant cold that's only going to get worse." Sarah changed the subject. He didn't mind. He learned early on that 'slow and steady wins the race' in the dating world.

Brandon laughed. "You really miss Florida, don't you?"

"Yes, the weather and my life as I knew it. But other than the temperature, Maine is growing on me. I just need my blood to thicken up again and I might be able to tolerate it."

Brandon reached in the back of his truck. "Until then, you can use this to keep warm. It's clean. I promise."

Her melodious laugh filled the cab of the truck like a group of songbirds on a warm summer morning.

She swam in his sweatshirt, but it did something to his insides seeing this beautiful woman wearing his clothes. The caveman within him awoke, and he wanted to claim her.

Ten minutes later, they arrived at his log cabin. "This is so cute."

Brandon puffed out his chest. "My house is not cute."

"But it is my brawny construction man."

Did he hear her right? *Her* construction man. If she kept talking like that, he'd have no choice but to kiss her.

"You know what I mean." She hid her face and reached for the door handle.

"Don't you move." Brandon said, hopping out of the cab. He jogged around the hood and opened her door. "Milady." He reached his hand out for hers.

"I think you have this high truck so you can help all your women in and out."

He pulled her to the ground. Mere inches between them, Brandon leaned around her shoulder and shut the door. Then he leaned into her hair and whispered, "You're the only woman special enough to ride in this truck. Unless you include my mom." Her body shivered again, as he kissed her cheek.

"Ready to watch a movie?" He asked, straightening to his full height?

"S-sure," she stammered, turning toward the cabin. Brandon placed his hand on her lower back, guiding her to the door.

Brandon is not a musical movie guy, but with Sarah by his side, he endured the Wizard of Oz. As a child, he watched it with his mother. Listening to Sarah sing each song and even state the lines verbatim with the actors was entertaining.

"You really love this movie, huh?"

She covered her face with her hands, laughing. "Maybe."

Brandon gently pulled her wrists. "I think it's cute." He bopped her on the nose. This woman had him acting like a lovesick teenager, his heart pounding in his chest and his palms sweating.

As Dorothy effectively doused the Wicked Witch of the West with a generous amount of water, Brandon, meanwhile, felt the heat intensely and wished for some water to alleviate the fire within him. With her thigh completely relaxed and resting against his, Sarah's proximity sent a jolt of exhilaration through him.

By the time Dorothy says her famous final line, "...oh, Auntie Em - there's no place like home," Brandon had prayed for self control at least ten times since they sat down.

"Thanks for watching that with me. I could tell it wasn't something you would have done on your own."

"Everything's better with you."

Sarah laughed. "That sounded better in your head, right?" She teased him with the same line he used before when he sounded too cheesy.

"Maybe. But it's still the truth." Sarah didn't move. Was she expecting him to do or say something?

Her ocean blue eyes were full of concern and she twisted her wedding ring around her finger.

"Sarah, I won't push you to do anything you don't want to. All I ask is don't give me mixed signals. My self-control is only so strong. I've been praying the entire movie for more." He shrugged slightly and smirked.

She nodded, but didn't say a word, so Brandon stood and held his hand out to her, helping her from the couch. "Are you ready to go home?"

"I-I don't think so."

Brandon rested his forehead against hers. "You didn't understand what I said about mixed signals, huh?"

She puffed out a hearty laugh. Brandon straightened to his full height. "It's not funny."

"I'm sorry." She ran her hands up his forearms, sending prickly sensations along his skin, leaving small, formed puckers in its wake. "I find you incredibly attractive and the more I get to know you, the more I like, but it's hard."

"Emotions usually are. Let's keep it simple. Can I please kiss you right now?"

Sarah nodded her head as her hands traveled to Brandon's shoulders, causing more tremors to shake his insides.

"Words please."

"Yes, Brandon, you can kiss me."

Without hesitation, Brandon captured her lips. Slow at first. He undid her ponytail and threaded his hands through her hair, cupping the back of her neck.

Once Sarah arched up, wrapping her arms around his neck, he tilted her head and deepened the kiss. The intoxicating warmth of her full lips sent a sensation through him that made his toes curl and his breath catch.

Their lips danced together while Brandon daydreamed about Sarah. If he got his way, this would be the delicious first taste of many more kisses. This wasn't one-sided; she responded with as much emotion as him. Her fingers played with the hair at the base of his neck.

She pulled away first. Eyes locked, they fought for breath, their chests rising and falling rapidly, the silence punctuated only by their labored breathing.

Her hand dropped to her stomach. He watched as she brought her finger to her mouth and nibbled on the tip of her nail. The awkward silence ate at him.

"You regret that?" He waited for her to say something. Anything.

She shook her head. "A little impulsive maybe."

What kind of answer was that? He'd waited weeks to kiss her. He might agree that he was reckless and took the kiss too far, but he'd never complain about tasting Sarah's lips.

Chapter 15

"I appreciate the opportunity. Give me a couple of days, and I'll let you know if I can make it work. Thank you."

Sarah slid her phone into her back pocket just as her dad entered the house with Brandon's arm slung over the back of his neck. The sky's dark gray clouds threaten to release any moment.

"Oh, my. What happened?"

Brandon sighed. "Ladders and fatigue don't go well together."

His dark eyes pinned Sarah. Her stomach, shoulders, and neck tightened. She rushed to the couch and pushed the pillows toward the back, giving him room to rest.

"Can I get you anything? Ibuprofen, maybe?"

He studied her. Would he refuse medicine just because she offered it? Certainly not. Brandon wasn't a fool.

"Two please." With a curt nod, she acknowledged his request, turned on her heels, and headed to the cupboard where her dad kept the medicine.

Gus hollered after her. "I have to tend to our last harvest. Do you need anything?"

"All set, Dad. Take it easy."

Sarah heard the storm door slam, announcing her dad's exit. That meant she was alone with Brandon. Ever since they kissed, things had been awkward. Because of her excessive guilt, no doubt.

She'd prayed, fasted, and prayed some more. She tried to rid herself of the ruefulness she felt about moving on without Jake. Every time she made a little progress, their proximity set her back. Her traitorous body, a constant reminder of how much his sweet words and soft touch affected her.

"Here, take these." Sarah dropped the pills into his hand, trying not to touch him, but their fingers brushed, sending the same prickly sensation through her arm that his touch always did.

"Thank you." With a feather-light touch, his fingers grazed hers as he reached for the water glass.

"Don't do that." Sarah sighed.

Brandon smiled. "What? Show you affection. Let you know I'm interested." His voice, soft and caring.

His kindness rendered Sarah speechless. Brandon didn't get mad when they spoke. She wanted him to get mad at her for not being able to free herself from these doubts.

"I'm not going anywhere. But I can't pretend you don't drive me crazy."

He swallowed the pills. Sarah's mouth dried, watching his Adam's apple shift up and down as he drank. Who found that appealing? Her.

"Will you sit and chat or do you have something you're doing?"

Sarah nodded and moved toward the empty chair next to the couch. His fingers gripped her wrist, stopping her. Brandon moved one of the back pillows and slid his hips over.

She slowly lowered her body to the spot he made for her.

"Kurt is crazy about Lily. He said it was okay if I told you because he wants you to like him."

"Aw, that's sweet."

"I told him to join the club," Brandon teased, draping his arm across her lap.

Sarah's fingers ran along his forearm. "I do like you, Brandon. That's the problem."

"Where I come from, that's not a problem." He tightened his hand on her hip. "I know you love God. When are you going to trust Him?"

"I do."

Brandon cleared his throat. "If you did, you wouldn't be wrestling with guilt."

"Uh!" Sarah sprang to her feet. "How dare you judge me!"

As she walked away from the couch, he called out, "In your anger, do not sin. Do not let the sun go down while you are still angry."

"Of course, you would throw the Bible in my face." Sarah stopped, but didn't turn around.

"That's not what I'm doing. But I know Christ would want us to work it out."

A vicious roar, like a lion's growl, reached her ears as torrential rain poured from the sky.

"Are you kidding me?" Sarah scoffed, gesturing toward the window.

"I am sorry that I got you so mad," Brandon began gently as he swung his legs to the floor.

"I'm not mad at you. I will be if you don't elevate that leg." Her voice, louder, so he could hear over the rain, but her grin hopefully told him she was teasing. When he saluted her, she figured he knew.

He waved her over. She complied, resting next to him again. "I'm probably going to make you mad again, but I'm feeling dangerous today."

Brandon was already dangerous in her mind. Would her heart be able to withstand this man much longer? She didn't think so.

"Jesus was the only perfect man on earth. I know Jake was amazing or you wouldn't have loved him, but he wasn't perfect and I'm sure you can think of a time you were upset with him. That doesn't make you love him any less." He brushed his thumb across her knuckles.

His words were the gentle reminder she needed.

"I'm not trying to make your life difficult, but I am hoping you'll give this imperfect man a chance to make you smile, take you to dinner, something." A mischievous glint in his eyes sparkled as he said, "I've been dying to kiss you again, but I think that's what made you pull away, so I'll keep my lips to myself if that helps."

A single teardrop ran down Sarah's face. Brandon straightened his back. "Don't cry." He pulled her in for a hug.

Meanwhile, Sarah's core lit up. She couldn't escape the Holy Spirit whispering in her head, Take a leap of faith. Trust me. Sarah surrendered and pressed her hands to his chest, creating room between them. "What if I don't want you to keep your lips to yourself?"

He blinked twice. "Is that what you're telling me, Sarah?"

"Yes." She sounded more confident than she felt. The power coming from within had nothing to do with her.

"Ahhh," she shrieked when Brandon hoisted her onto his lap and crashed his lips into hers. His arms roamed up and down her back, stopping only to cup her face.

"You are the most beautiful woman ever," he whispered, his breath warm against her lips. Then, pulling her tightly against his chest, he captured her lips again in a deep, lingering kiss.

His heart beat matched hers, a steady, strong pulse mirroring her own racing heart. With his lips parted in a silent invitation, he fully enticed her to explore the depths of his kiss and the new beginning it held.

"Whoa! Sorry." Sarah hopped off Brandon's lap at the sound of her dad's voice. She would have landed on the floor had it not been for Brandon wrapping his arms around her.

"Hi, Dad," Sarah casually whispered. The memory of Brandon's lips on hers still tingling.

"Well, if I knew all it would take to get you two together was a measly slip off a ladder, I would have pushed you weeks ago," Gus chortled.

"Real nice, Dad. We're not together." She looked at Brandon. "Are we?"

He smirked. "I don't make a habit of making out with women I'm not pursuing or dating."

That's vague. "Whatever we are, is between us." Sarah stormed out the door, realizing just then that it stopped raining at some point.

Before it shut, she heard her dad say, "Alright, it's about time. You treat her like Jesus would."

Sarah walked down the street to clear her head. For the first time, she didn't feel suffocated with guilt.

The warm sun worked its way through the clouds, a glorious gift from God washing over her as she prepared for this new chapter of her life to unfold.

CHAPTER 16

WHEN BRANDON OPENED THE door, he received a blast of, "Whatever, Mom! I'll never make the team. There's nowhere to practice." Brandon heard the yelling and thought about leaving before the ladies saw him.

"Lily, why can't you practice in the driveway?" Sarah suggested.

"Oh, right, Mom. The tar has cracks. Do you want me to break my ankle?" Lily retorted.

Sounding desperate to help Lily, she offered the only suggestion she could think of, "Listen Lily, what do you want me to do? Call someone to fix the driveway or drive you to the school gym every day. I want you on the team. But that's a bit much."

"Really, it's cold out there! Remember, you moved me to Maine."

Almost in tears, her voice quivered, "Oh, Lily, give me a break! I'm trying to help you!"

Brandon sensed Sarah's impending tears from her tone. He couldn't take it anymore. Seeing Sarah slouched in the kitchen chair, Brandon felt a quick twinge in his heart. He stepped in to offer a solution.

"I'm sorry. I couldn't help but overhear your argument." Brandon turned to Lily. "Yelling at your mother won't fix your problem, but I bet you have a Sunday school teacher who has connections and can reserve a gym for you."

Lily crossed her arms over her chest in a huff. "You're just trying to impress my mother. If you can shut me up, you think you'll gain points with her."

"Lily!" Sarah barked. "That's enough."

"You know I'm right."

Brandon waved off the comments as if they were no big deal. He didn't want either of them to think Lily's perception had merit.

"I do like your mother a lot. But I also like to help people, especially teens. If you ever want to practice, let me know."

She caught Brandon off guard with a spontaneous hug. "I'm sorry for my careless words." She pulled back and whispered. "I'm not sure how I feel about you two dating, but if she dates anyone, I'm glad it's you." A grin split her face before she ran upstairs.

Wow. He never expected that type of acceptance from Lily. She'd been attending Sunday school with Kurt for about a month, but remained quiet, listening to the other teens, so Brandon needed to learn more about her during their dinners.

Gus already gave him a standing invitation to dinner on the weekdays since he'd dedicated himself to getting the projects done. That meant twelve-hour days on the property.

Most days, he was able to focus on his work, but sometimes, flirting with Sarah took precedence. According to Gus, that was normal. For Brandon, it seemed reckless. He had a list of potential customers to call back. Eating lunch with Sarah had become more important than working during that hour.

"I'm shocked. Not only did you tame Lily the lion, you offered gym time during the wintertime. That's nearly impossible."

Brandon felt his cheeks flush hot and tingle with heat. Walking into the kitchen, he leaned down and pressed a lingering kiss to Sarah's cheek. "May I help with dinner? I wrapped up early. It's too dark."

"I'll never turn down help. Thank you."

Thirty minutes later, Brandon plated chicken marsala on four plates, while Lily set the rest of the table.

Gus said a prayer for their food and Brandon dug in. He had never cooked a meal like this. What for? Cooking for one was not nearly as fun as cooking for the family. Not that he was part of this family. He'd be lying if he said he didn't imagine that at least once a day.

What happened? He used to focus on his business. Would he ever be able to put her first? Without a doubt. Brandon followed the prayer closet Pastor Pete preached. God first, then family, church, and the world. If God gave him Sarah for a season, who was he to put his business above her?

"Tell me something about yourself Lily." Brandon stated, casually taking a bite of his chicken and moaning. "This is delicious."

Everyone laughed at him. He might have been a bit dramatic, but he wanted to show his appreciation to Sarah.

Lily put her fork down to answer Brandon's question. "Columbus Day weekend, the basketball coach is hosting another pre-season get fit practice. In order to make varsity, I have to run an eight-minute mile. I haven't run in months. What am I going to do?" Lily shrieked in fear.

Sarah clapped her hands. Bouncing in her seat, she grasped Lily's shoulder. "Perfect timing. I decided to train again as well. We can run together." Sarah's cheerful voice filled the room.

"Can we start tomorrow, Mom?" Lily pushed eagerly. "Wait, are you going to substitute?"

When Sarah hesitated, Lily persisted, "Mom, what aren't you telling us?"

"I turned down the full-time substitute position for this year, but I am on the sub list for a couple of days a week."

Gus mentioned Sarah dealing with her job situation. He wished she confided in him, but he reminded himself not to push her.

"We can start tomorrow," Sarah conceded.

She held back details. Brandon saw pain and unease in her eyes.

As usual, Sarah clammed up, allowing everyone around her to engage in conversation, only taking part with one-word answers, a simple laugh, or "Hm."

While she and Lily cleared the table, he and Gus cleaned the kitchen.

"Spill it," Gus ordered in a hushed whisper.

"I don't know what you're talking about," Brandon played dumb.

"You know what the Bible says about lying."

Yes, he did, but he wasn't sure what Gus wanted, so he carefully chose his words, revealing only what was necessary. Gus had already used that deceptive strategy once, leaving him feeling foolish.

"When are you going to do something about this tension between you and Sarah?"

"Me?"

Gus nodded.

Brandon remained quiet. Finally, he gave in. "I've made my intentions clear. Sarah's hot one minute and cold the next few days. I won't put more pressure on her."

"She needs people who won't give up on her," Gus declared.

Of course, she didn't need that. Had he given any sign he would? "It's not like I'm going anywhere."

"We're done. Do you guys need help?" Sarah bounded into the kitchen.

No, but Brandon didn't want her to leave, either. Gus apparently had the same idea as him.

"Lily, how about you teach your old grandpa how to use my phone better?"

Without waiting for her answer, Gus whisked his granddaughter away.

"He's not very subtle," Sarah said, taking the plate from Brandon and setting it in the dishwasher.

"No, but I'm glad I get time alone with you."

She smiled, but it didn't reach her eyes.

A silent tension permeated the room. Five minutes later, he rinsed the last dish. Once Sarah loaded it into the machine and shut the door, Brandon filled the space in front of her.

"I'm here to listen. You don't have to travel this world alone."

Sarah sighed. "It feels weird sharing my everyday life happenings with you."

That hurt, but at least she was being honest. Hoping he didn't regret it, he asked, "You don't want to, you mean?"

Sarah shook her head and hoisted herself on the counter. "I do. So many times today, I thought about finding you. I wanted to ask your opinion if I made the right decision or talk it out."

"Why didn't you." Brandon moved forward, resting his palms on her thighs. *Thank you, Lord, for this moment.*

"You were working, and I didn't want you to fall off a ladder again—"

He cut her off. "If I got the same care from my beautiful nurse as last time, I'd injure myself daily." She laughed. That was music to his ears. "I'm sorry. Continue."

"My emotions got the best of me and I fell into a funk."

Brandon pressed a lingering kiss to her forehead. "Sarah, I want you to talk to me, funk and all." He ran his hand through his hair, contemplating whether to push further. He had to know. "In my mind, we're dating. So I'm here for you. Through the blah moments and the exciting ones."

A few silent beats later, a surge of anticipation rolled through Brandon's body. "You're still willing to give us a try, right?"

She nodded. "Yes," Sarah said, resting her palms on his forearms. An instant warmth spread through him. It was then that he noticed her left ring finger, void of the wedding ring he'd seen before. *That's progress.*

Sarah must have felt something, too, because she pulled Brandon even closer. "Thank you for being patient with me."

He couldn't hold back the big smile filling his face. "Any time."

His lips clung to hers, igniting a passionate spark that spread between them. Sarah wrapped her arms around his shoulders and pulled him closer.

Not wanting Gus to catch them again, Brandon reluctantly pulled back. He pressed a chaste kiss to her lips and lifted her off the counter.

Wrapping her hand in his, he guided her to the couch. "Come, tell me about your day."

With her feet resting on his thigh, he massaged her calves. "I'm not sure if I want to teach in public schools anymore. You might think I'm crazy, but I'd love to go on a mission trip and teach kids English."

"You're not crazy at all. I've often wondered if I should have already been on a mission trip, helping rebuild places hit by natural disasters."

"You could work with teens, too. Your ability to bring Lily around so quickly... Amazing."

Brandon laughed. "I think Kurt gets most of the credit there."

"Probably. But, I won't leave Dad. Something doesn't seem right with him, and I'm not talking about grief. He gets winded easily."

"Yeah, I noticed that as well, recently."

Sarah nodded. "I guess we'll have to keep an eye on him."

"Yup. But I have to admit. I'd rather keep my eye on you." Brandon leaned down, his elbow pressing in on the cushion, so he didn't crush her. Sarah let out a cute giggle. Their legs entwined. He descended slowly, brushing the hair away from her eyes. "God blessed me richly when you entered my life."

He showered her jaw with kisses before claiming her mouth. She ran her fingers through his hair, sending a tingling sensation throughout him. He'd never experienced anything like this before. Yeah, he'd dated women and had his share of kissing, but this was more. Sarah reached his soul. He sighed a moan into her mouth.

"You drive me insane."

Time escaped him as he kissed Sarah. Like two ragged breathed teenagers, they explored each other. When Brandon reached his limit, he pulled back, resting his head on her forehead. "I have to go home or I won't be in the good graces of my Savior anymore."

Sarah giggled again.

"Don't laugh at me."

Sarah hurried to answer. "Oh, I'm not. Thank you for being such a gentleman." She cupped his face and pressed a lingering kiss to his lips, initiating another deep moan.

He hopped off the couch, righted his shirt, and helped Sarah to her feet. With her hand secured in his, Brandon led her to the doorway where he laced up his work boots.

Straightening, he laced their fingers together again. "Any chance I get to see you this weekend?"

Sarah thought for a second. "Definitely at church. Tomorrow, I promised Lily we'd run.

"Be safe."

She smiled and nodded.

He gave her a light kiss on the lips. "Good night," he murmured, the taste of her breath a sweet memory.

"Night."

As Brandon drove home, he realized his dad was wrong. He could have it all. He'd have the business he wanted and the woman he wanted. As long as Sarah didn't change her mind.

CHAPTER 17

REACHING THE MILE MARKER, Lily was five seconds short of making the varsity team.

"You'll have no problem shaving your time down," Sarah encouraged her daughter.

She and Lily hadn't raced in ages, so they jogged along, chatting about the past.

"I can't believe I've run a marathon before," Lily huffed and puffed.

"I remember when you ran for the first time. You couldn't run a quarter mile. Your dad and I took turns walking with you until you increased your running stamina." Sarah, winded herself, smiled at the memory.

"The PE teacher said there's a race on November 25th that starts at the high school. It's called Burn off the Turkey 5k. Do you want to run together?" Lily asked.

"Yeah," Sarah shook her head.

"Will you train for Boston again?" The sympathy in Lily's eyes stunned Sarah.

When Jake died a few weeks after her qualifying race, Sarah lost her desire to run. She didn't know if she would ever get back to that level of running without Jake to push her and run with her.

"I don't know. Your dad was a big part of my running. He helped, encouraged, and pushed me to do my best. I don't have anyone to hold me accountable now," Sarah said in a discouraged tone.

Brandon would probably run with you.

"Not you, too, Lily."

"It was just a thought."

Thankfully, Lily dropped the subject. She shared her fondest childhood memory. "I still can't believe you and dad let me sit on the alligator at Gator World. I still remember accidentally touching his fang, and it was sharp. I don't think I would do that now."

"It had a band around its jaw," Sarah defended herself.

Sarah reminisced about the countless times they went to theme parks, orange groves, and beaches while Lily was a child. "Remember when your dad threw us in the water at Coco Beach in the middle of January? It was pretty cold for Florida."

Lily laughed. Then she stopped walking and looked at her mom. "We haven't talked about Dad in a very long time. This is really nice."

As they returned to the driveway, Sarah softly replied, "It's really hard to talk about him. I miss him so much. The only person I love more than your dad is you!" Sarah leaned over and hugged Lily so tight that her daughter needed to break free for a breath. She felt reconnected with Lily for the first time since arriving in Maine.

Ever since Lily and Kurt started dating, she never missed church. That made it easy on Sarah. Less fighting. Any tiffs were Lily hurrying Sarah out the door. This Sunday hadn't been any different. Still, Gus got them to church on time for Sunday School.

Lily lit up when she entered the sanctuary, and Kurt strolled toward her. "Morning, Mrs. Morris."

Sarah flinched. "Hi, Kurt. Please call me Sarah."

"I don't think I can do that," he remarked, causing a smile to form across her lips. "You're a good guy."

Brandon snuck up behind her, wrapping an arm around her back, resting his palm on her hip. "Morning beautiful," he said before dropping a chaste kiss on the top of her head.

"Let's go Kurt. It doesn't bother me that they're together, but I don't need to see it." Her tone was teasing, like any other teenager would use in the same situation. Sarah was proud of herself when she didn't let her mind read more into the comment.

"Save me a seat?" he asked as they headed in opposite directions for their respective classes.

"Sure," she said with a grin. He winked at her before turning and jogging off, probably knowing it wasn't a great idea to leave a room full of teenagers unsupervised.

The fall ambiance of the church drew Sarah in as she made her way to her class. The maroon and rich purple mums on the church steps welcomed God's family into the church. A fall basket overfilled with gourds, squash, and pumpkins was among the items near the altar. Pastor Pete's light green shirt underneath his charcoal suit jacket reminded Sarah of Maine's autumn beauty.

Most of all, she couldn't stop the giddy feeling in her chest from that quick encounter with Brandon.

Pastor Pete's sermon ended minutes ago, but the words still lingered in Sarah's mind as she sat lost in thought, the quiet murmur of the church fading into a contemplative silence. The Bible verse, "For my thoughts are not your thoughts, neither are your ways my ways," echoed quietly in her heart.

"Are you okay?" Brandon asked, rubbing his thumb along her shoulder like he had sporadically throughout the entire sermon.

Pastor Pete's message made Sarah realize it was time she accepted the fact that God wanted her here and she needed to appreciate His gifts. She studied Brandon. The care in his voice had her heart soaring. Sarah pictured a life with him, filled with sparks, laughter, and lots of kisses.

"Yeah. Everything's great." Sarah rested her hand on Brandon's thigh. She looked over her shoulder, finding her dad talking with Barbara. Lily and Kurt were chatting in the last pew. "Would you like to come for lunch and a run?"

"Are you asking me for a date?" Brandon slid even closer. He nuzzled his nose into her neck and dropped a chaste kiss on her jaw.

"Don't let it go to your head." She tapped him on the cheek with her palm.

"How about I grab some Italians on the way home for us?"

Sarah shook his head. "I invited you to lunch. You don't need to buy lunch."

"I have a bigger plan in mind, if that's okay." He eyed the back of the sanctuary.

"Whatever you want." Sarah snickered.

Brandon stood, holding his hand out to Sarah. They walked hand-in-hand to the exit. "Barbara, Kurt, would you like to join us for sandwiches at Gus's?"

How did she get so lucky? This man kept getting better and better.

CHAPTER 18

As BRANDON DROVE TO the sandwich shop, his mind couldn't escape Pastor's words. "Hey Brandon, are you letting God take control, or are you still resisting?"

Brandon realized it was time he accepted the fact that God wanted him in Sarah's life and released the relationship over to Him. He also asked God to show him how to grow his business and have Sarah in his life at the same time.

His phone rang and Brandon sighed when his dad's name splayed across the screen in his car. Pressing the phone button, he greeted his dad. "Hey, what's up?"

"Please tell me that's not how you answer the phone for customers."

"Do you have work for me, Dad? I figured you'd still fix things up yourself."

His dad hissed at him. "Don't get smart with me." Brandon thought he heard his mom laughing in the background.

"What can I do for you, Dad?"

"Don't mind him, honey. He's grumpy because he's not working."

Funny. Since Sarah arrived, Brandon noticed he'd been in a better mood around her, not the other way around.

"Hey, Mom."

"You sound happier than I've ever heard you. Have you met a woman?"

How did she always know? Brandon's silence only confirmed her theory.

"We need to have you over for dinner."

"Don't encourage that, Evelyn. Brandon needs to focus on the business. He can't go falling in love and dropping customers to spend time with some woman."

What a jerk!

"Alright. It's been great chatting, but I have things to do with my woman. Talk later." As Brandon hung up, he heard his mom telling Caleb to stop putting pressure on him. "You tell him, Mom," Brandon said aloud to the empty cab and silent phone, realizing his dad never told him why he'd called. Oh, well.

After lunch, Kurt and Lily shot hoops in the driveway, Gus and Barbara sat on the porch swing, and Brandon and Sarah hit the pavement.

Once they reached the three-mile mark of their four-mile loop, Sarah slowed to a brisk walk for a cooldown. With her fingers laced and resting on top of her head, she let out a few deep breaths. "You can keep running. You don't have to wait for me."

"That's okay, this was an extra run for me," Brandon said. A warmth spread through him when Sarah's eyes softened, catching what he said. "I wanted to run with you."

As they crossed the street, it left Sarah on the outside. He wrapped his arm around her waist, guiding her to the inside.

"That was thoughtful. Thank you."

"You haven't figured it out by now?"

"What?" her eyes peered up at him.

He wrapped his arm around her shoulders. "I will do anything to protect you."

His phone interrupted the sweet moment. Pulling it out, he announced, "It's a text from Lily."

"Oh?"

He read it quickly. "She asked if I'd take her and Kurt to the gym tonight." She nodded. A confident grin spread across his face as he asked, "Do you think your knee is up for a little basketball?"

"You're on!"

CHAPTER 19

ON THE WAY HOME from the gym, Sarah rubbed her knee.

"You should have let them have the bucket."

Sarah shrugged. "I know. It's easy to say, but in the moment, the idea of my daughter beating me on the court... I wasn't ready for that."

"What about you?"

"Me?"

Sarah chuckled. "Whose head were you envisioning as the ball?"

A grim smirk grazed his lips. A zing of guilt shot through her as she waited for him to answer. She never should have said anything.

"I'm sorry. You don't have to answer."

Brandon reached out for her hand. "Forgive me. I'll tell you anything. I was trying to control my response."

She'd never seen Brandon upset like this. What could make this calm man upset?

"I heard from my parents today. When I told them about you, my dad pushed the business again, but my mom wants to meet you."

He told them about her? His dad must see her as a villain, stealing his son away from him.

"I'm sorry if I caused any trouble between you and your dad."

He squeezed her hand. "You did nothing wrong. He finds fault with anything or anyone when my attention wavers from the business for a second."

"Am I a distraction, Mr. Taylor?" her voice, low and sultry. Her flirting took her by surprise.

His eyes sparked with playfulness. "You know you are."

"In all seriousness, has your business suffered since I moved back?"

Brandon shook his head. "No. I got behind on some calls, but I'm caught up now and I've got steady work scheduled between now and into the new year."

"So, what's his problem?" Sarah asked, not understanding what Caleb expected from his son.

He snorted. "Caleb Taylor put business over basketball games, parent-teacher conferences, date nights with mom, everything. He expects the same from me."

"What do you want?" Sarah asked softly.

He didn't answer for a few beats. Then one, single word slipped from his lips in a barely there whisper that she may have missed if she wasn't studying him.

"You."

Her pulse raced out of control and her inner teenage self released a deep sigh. Heat rushed up her neck and settled in her cheeks when Brandon brought their linked hands to his lips and kissed her knuckles.

How could he be so sure after only a couple of months? Sarah hadn't been the easiest to deal with. She had to pray every night to drop the guilt she'd harbored since she started thinking of Brandon in a romantic way.

"Did I scare you?"

Maybe.

CHAPTER 20

THE SCHOOL BUS DROPPED Lily off and she bolted up the driveway. Running off the bus was abnormal for a high school student, so Brandon stopped her. "Is everything okay?"

Sarah met them in the driveway. "What's up, Lily?"

"Everything is wonderful," she exclaimed with a ragged breath. "Kurt asked me to the winter dance." Can I go please?" Lily clasped her hands together in a begging fashion.

"Did you already tell him yes?" Sarah questioned.

"No, not really. I said yes, unless you said no," Lily replied as she loosened her hands.

"I'll think about it," Sarah informed her daughter while she entered the kitchen to start dinner. "When is it?"

"It's the Friday after Thanksgiving. The school hosts a whole evening of dancing and all the money they earn goes to the shelter in town to help replenish their shelves after the Thanksgiving Day rush. Lily explained.

"Oh, I chaperone that every year because it's for a great cause." Brandon said.

"Since it's for a good cause, I'm fine with you going, as long as you don't mind me chaperoning," Sarah replied.

"Great, my mom and Sunday school teacher are going to be spying on me," Lily sighed. "If that's what it takes, fine. But please, both of you don't embarrass me," Lily pleaded.

"So you mean I can't dress up like Scott Hamilton and glide around the floor with your mom twirling above my head?" Brandon joked.

"Scott who?" Lily questioned.

"Now you're showing your age," Sarah laughed at him. "Remember, Lily grew up in Florida. Watching ice skating isn't something we did for fun there. We bathed in the sun and laughed at all of the fools who lived in areas cold enough for ice." Sarah explained sarcastically. "I guess we are those fools now, Lily," Sarah added.

"That's fine by me. I like it here in Maine. I'm glad you moved us here, Mom." Lily hugged her mom and gave her a kiss on the cheek. "I'm going to call Kurt."

For the next two hours, Lily floated around like that Disney princess who sang and birds made her dress. Her excitement continued on through dinner. When he finished, Gus cleared his plate and excused himself.

As Brandon was getting ready to leave, Lily asked to talk with him. "We'll just be a couple of minutes, Mom." He saw rejection and hurt in Sarah's face. Lily must have, too. She said, "It's boy stuff, Mom. I'd ask Dad if he was here."

Ouch! Brandon shrugged, letting Sarah know he didn't know anything about this. When the two of them returned, he saw Sarah quickly wiped the tears from her eyes.

He wanted to stay and talk to her. Would she open up? One thing he'd learned about Sarah was that if she didn't want to talk, she wouldn't.

Brandon put his jacket on to leave. "Thank you for another great meal, Sarah."

She acknowledged his compliment with a half-hearted smile, but continued to wash the table. Would Sarah really be upset that Lily wanted to talk to him? Lily had started sharing more during Sunday School. Besides, everyone knew his interest in Sarah. She must have expected Lily to share things with him eventually. He'll never be her dad, but he had a strong desire to watch out for her.

As Brandon was about to leave, Lily ran over and gave him a quick hug and thanked him for their talk. "You're welcome." He whispered, "I bet your mom would love to talk with you about this, too." She eyed Sarah and nodded.

"I'm heading upstairs to finish my homework, Mom."

"Okay." Sarah replied, grabbing her coat. Turning toward Brandon, she asked, "Can we talk outside?"

Whipping around at Brandon as she closed the door behind her, Sarah scoffed, "Why is Lily talking to you? You're not her dad."

Brandon chose to ignore that hurtful comment, knowing the amount of pain Sarah felt.

Placing a hand on Sarah's shoulder; he replied, "Settle down, Sarah. She wanted to know what a guy's actions meant, that's all."

Now crying, Sarah wiped her face with her jacket sleeve. "But that's not all. I am her mom and I want her to turn to me."

Sitting Sarah down on the porch swing, Brandon knelt in front of her and placed his hands on her thighs and reassured her that she was a good mom, but she wasn't a guy and couldn't explain why guys did certain things. Brandon promised to share everything with her as long as Lily said he could. "I have Lily's best interest at heart. Even though I'm not her dad, I'll be like a big brother watching out for her."

Sarah smiled. "Thank you. I don't want her to get hurt." The two stared into each other's eyes for what seemed like an eternity.

"I don't want that either. If you trust me a little more, you'll see that I won't hurt you either."

Sarah cupped his face. "Thank you for being patient with me. I don't think before I speak sometimes. We're really lucky to have you."

We're. She included herself. Brandon leaned closer. "No, I'm the lucky one." He pressed a soft kiss to her lips.

He led her back to the door and kissed her cheek. "Good night, beautiful Sarah." He turned and bounded down the stairs, his heart soaring. Sarah had finally let her guard down.

CHAPTER 21

SARAH RAN WITH LILY until she shaved her time and made varsity. But since then, she hadn't seen her daughter very much. Lily's demanding basketball schedule left her with little free time, which she set aside for Kurt.

Tying her shoes, while she balanced the phone between her ear and shoulder, Sarah said, "I don't want to be late, so I'll talk to you later, Jill."

She and Jill were building their friendship again. Jill repeatedly apologized for helping set her up with Brandon at the movies. How could she be mad about that? It may have bothered her then, but it didn't anymore.

When Sarah left for Lily's game, Gus and Brandon were still trying to finish up the project for the day, but hoped to make it. With it scheduled to snow at least three more inches overnight, they scurried, like squirrels gathering acorns, to complete their outside renovations.

Sarah arrived as the teams matched up. At five feet seven inches, Lily won the tip and the home team fans on the left side of the court cheered.

Quietness came quickly though when their point guard, a cute little brunette, threw the ball out of bounds instead of faking the pass and getting it to Lily on the weak side. Sarah waited for the visiting team to in-bound the ball. Then she briskly walked along the baseline to sit behind the player's bench.

Sarah loved watching Lily play basketball and got teary-eyed when she remembered how Lily, Jake, and she would play basketball for hours. When the referee blew his whistle, it brought Sarah's mind back to the game. She eyed the empty space next to her. The hole in her heart that she tried to close popped a stitch when she realized this was the first game she watched Lily play without Jake at her side.

The crowd cheered, pulling Sarah back into the game. Lily performed an amazing box out and threw a precise outlet pass to the opposite foul line to her teammate for the easy layup.

Lily was having a spectacular game. At the end of the first, she had twelve points, ten rebounds, and three assists. Between quarters, while the coach spoke, Sarah glanced back and forth—observing Kurt's loving look at Lily and the door, where she hoped to see her dad and Brandon.

Sarah became engrossed in the game. The score went back and forth as the teams swapped basket for basket, foul for foul. Both teams were accurate with their shots. Sarah knew the last seven minutes of the game would hinge on turnovers and missed opportunities.

She could tell that Lily was getting tired. Her box out looked weak and her defense suffered. Sarah always helped Lily by telling her the time left in the quarter or game and the score. "Hey fifteen," referring to Lily's number, "You have five minutes—keep solid D." Sarah instantly noticed Lily's defense returned to normal.

Sarah's attention to the game forced her to miss her dad and Brandon enter the gymnasium. As the two men climbed the bleachers, Sarah acknowledged them with a wide-mouth smile. She found herself captivated by Brandon's charm and striking appearance once more. The clean jeans and polo shirt that stressed every muscle he had caught her eye.

She turned her focus back on the game when the referee blew his whistle.

"A nail biter, aye?" Gus said as he and Brandon sat on either side of Sarah.

"How's she doing?" Brandon rested his elbows on his knees, studying the court.

She nodded and squirmed in her seat as the game neared the end. The tension was palpable as Lily stepped to the foul line with only three-tenths of a second remaining; the squeak of her shoes on the polished floor echoing in the silent gym. Lily shot, and Sarah felt a chill run down her spine, knowing it was short. The ball bounced off the front of the rim.

"Come on, Lily. You got this. Don't send it into overtime." Sarah clasped her hands together and brought them to her lips.

"Does the other team have any timeouts?" Brandon asked.

"Nope."

Before the referee passed the ball to Lily, Sarah heard a voice in the crowd yell, "Come on Lily, you can do this!" Kurt stood with his hands clasped, a nervous energy radiating from him.

Lily shot and the ball bounced off the back of the rim, then the front of the rim and finally it fell through the net. Sarah jumped out of her seat, clapping and cheering.

The other team snatched the ball and inbounded it. The guard's wild shot echoed through the stadium as it bounced off the backboard, the scoreboard's buzzer sounding in sync. *Thank you, Lord! I know this won't happen all the time, but this was a great win for her!*

While Sarah waited for Lily to come out of the locker room, Gus got restless and asked if she minded if he left with her car.

"I'm sure Brandon won't mind bringing you ladies home, would you?" Gus slapped Brandon on the back.

Brandon smiled at Sarah. "I'd love to," he replied.

As her dad headed out of the gym, Sarah yelled to him, "Please call me when you get home, Dad."

"Okay." Gus waved his hand and shut the gym door.

Sarah sat on the first bleacher and rested her elbows on her knees. Her heart started fluttering when he sat next to her. Their legs rested against each other and Brandon gently ran his hand over her back, as she rested her head in her hands.

"Are you okay?" Brandon sounded concerned.

"My dad didn't look good. He's been working too hard lately." Sarah straightened up, forcing Brandon's arm to fall off her back. "Are the renovations almost done?"

"I can finish things up on my own," Brandon informed her as he rested his forearms on his thighs. "Well, I might need some help from you." He looked back at her and added a smile.

Sarah couldn't tell if his request for help was genuine or a ploy to be near her. The scent of his cologne and the warmth of his smile made it so she didn't mind. "I'll help you, but it will cost you," she teased.

Before Brandon could respond, Lily came rushing out of the locker room. "Mom, can I go with the team to get ice cream? Kurt is going too, so he can bring me home."

Sarah wasn't comfortable with her daughter riding with Kurt before, but she came home safe. The pressure to make a quick decision bore down on her like a heavy weight pressing on her chest only made it worse. She worried about her daughter getting hurt or worse—a fatal car accident and never being able to see Lily again. The same familiar voice she sometimes heard while praying at night entered her head. *She'll be okay, I've got her. Remember, she's mine—I lent her to you.*

She tried to ignore the voice, but it got louder and louder as she stared at her wonderful daughter. At an early age, Sarah taught her daughter not to beg and plead for things, or the answer would be no. She was thankful for that now, as Lily stood in front of her with an eager look, waiting for the answer.

"Ya know, Sarah, the snow went out to sea, so that's one less thing to worry about." Brandon supported Lily's request with his own agenda in mind.

"Okay, you can go. But you need to be home by ten. Deal?" Sarah stood and squeezed Lily like she would never see her again.

Lily agreed and ran back into the locker room, while Sarah stood staring at the door her daughter disappeared behind.

"Looks like it's you and me. Brandon sounded like a kid in a candy store. When she didn't say anything, Brandon walked to her and placed his hands on her shoulders. "She's going to be okay."

She nodded, only half believing his words.

Brandon led her out of the gymnasium with one arm around her shoulders, and she leaned into him. He didn't remove his arm until he opened the truck door for her. Once Sarah got settled, Brandon shut the door and ran around the front of the truck to the driver's side.

"Do you want dessert?"

"That does sound good, but I want to be home in case anything happens." What could she do once disaster had struck? Answer the phone? She knew how silly that sounded, but she appreciated that Brandon didn't dismiss her feelings.

"Are you sure I can't persuade you?"

She hesitated.

Brandon took a left hand turn. "We're heading to the diner."

Ten minutes later, they were sitting across from one another when Brandon gestured for her to order. "I'll have a hot fudge sundae with black raspberry ice cream, please."

He ordered a mini chocolate chip caramel sundae and thanked the waitress.

"So Kurt is responsible, right?"

Brandon chuckled. "Very. In class we've discussed how to treat the opposite sex and not to have *that* until you're married."

Sarah rolled her eyes. "Once a boy always a boy."

The waitress arrived with their desserts and extra napkins. "This looks delicious," Sarah said, digging through the whipped cream. "Hmmmm."

"I'm glad you're enjoying it." Brandon sniggered as he sampled his own ice cream.

For the next fifteen minutes, they talked about Brandon's old girlfriends and how his dad didn't approve of any of them either.

"Is he going to fight with me at Thanksgiving?" Sarah asked, taking her last bite, placing her spoon in her dish, and sliding it to the end of the table to join Brandon's empty container.

"Not if I can help it."

Her heart skipped a beat. Is there anything better than a man who defends you? No.

"Let's get out of here. The weather men don't know what they're talking about. It's starting to snow."

Panic struck Sarah's chest and regret hung air as she gasped for breath. "You said it wasn't going to snow. Now Lily could be in danger."

Brandon pulled her to her feet. "Settle down, Sarah. Trust that God has her."

Sarah's hand covered her next gasp. "My dad never called me when he got home. We have to go now." She darted for the door.

Brandon dropped two twenties on the table and ran after Sarah. "Wait." He rushed to meet her at the truck, and the sound of the wet hinges creaking echoed as he opened it for her.

Sarah couldn't help but think she'd been irresponsible tonight and now her dad and daughter would pay for it.

Chapter 22

"I'M SURE HE'S FINE," Brandon insisted, trying to convince Sarah that her dad probably just forgot to call her.

"He didn't look good. Maybe he didn't make it home." Sarah's voice rose in panic.

Brandon frowned; his heart sad for Sarah. Lord, please rid her of the worry enveloping her. Half a mile from her home, Brandon accelerated, hoping Sarah would see the roads weren't that bad.

As they pulled into the driveway where Sarah's car rested, he saw the tension roll off her as she let out a breath.

Before Brandon could get Sarah's door open for her, she had already released her belt and dashed for the door. He followed her, praying she was worrying for nothing.

"He always turns the outside light on." Sarah fumbled with her keys.

Pressing his chest to her back, Brandon wrapped his arms around her. "I've got you." He placed his hands around Sarah's, taking the keys from her and unlocking the door.

She pushed through his embrace, flipping on all the lights as she ran to her dad's room. Brandon followed behind.

"Is everything okay?" he asked as she exited Gus's room, shutting the door with a whisper of a click.

She nodded. "The rise and fall of his chest is steady. I've never seen him this tired. Something is wrong. I can feel it." She blew out a breath. "I'm sorry. Did I sound like a nutcase?" Sarah asked, walking downstairs and plopping on the couch.

"You care about your family, there's nothing wrong with that." Brandon wanted to say more, but wasn't sure how far to push her. When Sarah remained silent, Brandon continued. "God's got them."

Sarah's eyes studied him. Did she believe in God's power like him?

"God is watching over both your dad and Lily right now. He's the only one who can truly protect them. You need to trust God to take care of your family."

She nodded. "I know that. Try telling my irrational side that."

"Any time she's up for listening, I'm here." Sarah chuckled at his silly answer.

"Lily won't be home for about an hour. I have an idea to pass the time. Are you in?" Brandon said, sliding closer to Sarah, wrapping his arm around her shoulders.

"Sure."

He dropped a kiss on the top of her head. "Perfect." Brandon sprang from the couch, pulling Sarah with him.

"Wait, what did I agree to?" Skepticism dripped from her lips.

Brandon's heart soared, a sudden burst of elation stopping him in his tracks.

"Oof. Sorry," Sarah squeaked when she plowed into the back of him.

"What were you expecting, Sarah?" Brandon brushed a rogue strand of hair behind her ear, pleased with the blush that filled her cheeks. His finger traced the delicate curve of her jaw, lingering on the soft skin. Brandon's ghostlike breath against her ear carried the whispered question, "Were you expecting this?" He trailed soft kisses down her neck, each one raising goosebumps on her skin. "I'm glad to see I can affect you like that." He rubbed his palms along her arms to warm her. "But I have a different plan."

"Uh," Sarah let out a little sigh. Her pouty lips and pleading eyes were almost too hard to ignore. He pressed a lingering kiss to her lips. "We'll have time for that after."

Ten minutes later, Sarah let out a belly laugh and collapsed to the floor. "This isn't fair."

"Don't be a sore sport. Start again. You spin first."

"We need a third person for this." She swiped the cardboard spinner off the floor. "What if you put socks on? Even the playing field."

"Spin, Sarah," he chuckled.

"Fine. Left leg, blue." She handed him the spinner.

"Right leg, yellow."

"Right hand, red," Sarah sighed.

They spun and moved until they resembled pretzels. Unable to hold her position, Sarah fell to the floor, laughing.

Brandon was right there, arms extended on either side of her. "I am the Twister champ."

"Sorry, I don't have a ribbon for you," Sarah's breathy response kicked Brandon's heart up a notch.

He inched down until their breath mingled. "That's okay. I don't want a ribbon."

"No? What do you want then?"

"This." Brandon crashed into her lips. The palpable attraction between them continued to grow. She wound her arms around his waist, pulling him closer. Now, on his forearms, he whispered, "Hello there."

"Sorry, I figured you were strong enough to hold yourself up, Champ."

"Oh, really?" Brandon tickled her sides while Sarah struggled to break free.

"My dad is sleeping. Please. Can't. Breathe."

Brandon's insides were bursting like fireworks. Sarah made him smile and laugh. He loved to tease her and joke with her. But when she wrapped her arms around him, he was putty in her hands. It was too early for Sarah to hear his feelings. He may have only known her for a couple of months, but this had to be love.

"Brandon, are you okay?"

"Yeah, I'm fine." She cupped her hand to his cheek anyway and studied his eyes.

If she looked long enough, she'd see his feelings. He broke their gaze when he hopped to his feet and held out his hand. "Come on, walk me to the door."

After many goodnight kisses, Brandon left; however, he needed to make a stop before going home.

CHAPTER 23

SARAH TRIED TO READ a book while she waited for Lily to get home, but her mind kept drifting to Brandon. His cologne, a woodsy scent mixed with vanilla, lingered in her hair. Her lips still tingled, remembering how Brandon's final kiss of the evening left her breathless.

Headlights reflected off the wall, signally a vehicle pulling into the driveway. Checking her watch, Lily wasn't due home for another twenty minutes. But a quick glance out the window confirmed Kurt brought her home early.

A truck crawled by the house, much slower than Sarah expected. The hairs on the back of her neck prickled. Worried about Lily, she opened the door.

"Mom! What are you doing?" Lily huffed.

"Did you see that truck?"

Kurt smiled while Lily pursed her lips. "Yeah, Brandon's spied on us for the last hour."

Dumbfounded, Sarah looked at Kurt for a different answer. Nope. He nodded, still smiling, as if he found it amusing.

"I'm sorry. I knew nothing about it. Drive safely, Kurt." Sarah turned her attention to her daughter. "See you in a few minutes."

Should she text Brandon and find out what he was thinking? Surprise still ran through her veins. Did he check on Lily because he was nervous, too? Or was he trying to help her relax? No, that couldn't be it. How could she rest if he didn't tell her what he was doing?

When Lily came in a few moments later, they discussed her game. "I am so proud of you. Your hustle, your accuracy... You lead the team tonight."

"Thanks."

"Kurt was adorable when he cheered for you. He's really supportive, huh?" Lily blushed.

"He reminds me of how Dad used to cheer you on at your races."

Sarah squeezed her lips together and nodded. "If that's the case, you better hold on to that one." Sarah cleared her throat, hoping to cover the emotion rising within.

"Brandon's like them, too," Lily said softly, covering her mom's hand with hers.

Lily spoke the truth. Sarah's lack of recognition felt like a glaring oversight. When would she give Brandon the credit he deserved?

"Brandon must really like you to check up on me. Or you nagged him so badly he wanted to shut you up." Lily belted out laughter, knowing all too well how her mother's mind worked.

"I plead the fifth," Sarah stated firming, but softened her lips long enough to smile. "You head up to bed and I'll lock up."

Lily began walking towards the stairs before turning back. "I asked Brandon when I should expect Kurt to kiss me, so maybe he was spying on me to see if it happened."

"What did he say?" Sarah folded her arms and twisted her foot to the side. Conflicting emotions rushed through Sarah. How could her daughter trust Brandon so quickly? The thought surprised her. She shouldn't be upset about this again. Sarah ebbed and flowed worse than the ocean?

"He told me to be patient and wait for God's timing."

Sarah just smiled and gave her daughter a hug. "Sounds like solid advice." Lily stared into her eyes. She saw the trouble holding Sarah hostage. Not helpful. Lily would never let this go now.

"Dad knows you love him. He'll be okay with you dating Brandon. Let him all the way into your world." Lily encouraged her with a nod. "Think about it. Dad can't protect you, but Brandon can. Dad would want you safe. Just like Brandon watched over me tonight."

Sarah shifted from one foot to the other. Why did her daughter have to know her so well?

"Mom, can I pray for us?"

Sarah nodded, moving toward her daughter. They linked hands and bowed their heads.

"Thank you, Lord, for this amazing day. We won our game, I got to spend time with Kurt, and I saw Brandon as the protector You created him to be. Help Mom to see you've given her another chance to share her life with someone who'll help keep us safe. Oh, yeah, and if you could hurry Kurt along, I'd like my first kiss. Thanks again. In Jesus' name, amen."

Chapter 24

Snow, a constant threat to construction schedules, didn't deter Brandon, accustomed to weather disrupting his work. But why this day?

The threat of snow pulled Brandon from Gus's list of projects to another job that needed his immediate attention. Mrs. Randall's son broke her window with a football. Though the window replacement would be a quick half-day job, he missed seeing Sarah's smile that brought him comfort throughout the day.

While he finished his breakfast, his phone rang. He groaned.

"Hi, Dad."

"Hi, honey, I'm on your dad's phone."

Perfect. Not having to deal with his dad this morning already started off better than expected.

"Your dad and I are on our way to breakfast."

His dad was there. Bummer. Maybe he would have mercy and not harass Brandon.

"Gus invited us for Thanksgiving dinner. Did you know about that?"

"Of course. If he's dating Gus's daughter, he knows. Hopefully, he isn't ignoring customers like he does us."

Do not engage with his babyish comments. Brandon wished he knew, but that would have required Sarah to invite him herself.

"No, I wasn't aware, Mom. I've been focused on work." He wasn't lying, but he didn't mention that part of his work was getting Sarah to let her guard down and trust him. If his dad knew that, he'd tell Brandon to ditch her because she was too much trouble.

"Oh. Well, we accepted, figuring—"

Brandon interrupted. "It's not a problem. I just didn't know." The possibility of rejection hung over his head like a rain cloud, ready to unleash a plethora of humiliation. No. Gus would invite him. Would he desire to go if Sarah didn't invite him? Yes. He was a glutton for punishment.

His promised patience wavered when they kissed. She lit a fire in him, testing his self-control. A fierce battle raged within him. The three words, I love you, threatened to spill from his lips every time he saw her, but he kept them captive. If he told Sarah he loved her, she'd run back to Florida on foot. Hopefully not.

"Mom, I have to get on the road—"

"You haven't left yet? Evelyn, hang up with the boy, so he can work."

I'm a man.

"I'll see you at Thanksgiving. Love you, Mom." He ended the call and let out a frustrated sigh.

As he pulled into the job site, his phone pinged with a text from Sarah.

Thanks for making sure Lily was safe last night.

An intense ache filled his chest, a desperate yearning to hold her close.

He waited to respond as three dots waved along the screen.

> We haven't discussed this, but Thanksgiving is next week. Do you already have plans, or would you like to eat with us?

His initial reaction was to respond right away. Instead, he counted backwards from one hundred. He didn't want to seem too eager. He only reached seventy-nine before his thumbs flew across the screen.

> You're welcome, and I'd love to spend Thanksgiving with you.

He added the wink emoji, but refrained from sending the one with hearts all around or the one blowing a heart kiss. His emotions were getting out of hand.

> Perfect. Maybe you'll arrive at seven and help me cook?

He threw his fist in the air. More time with Sarah is all he'd wanted and now his prayer was being answered. Thank you, Lord.

> Sure.

> As soon as I install this window, I'll swing by. It's starting to snow. Be safe if you go out.

He hit send before he could change his words. He wanted Sarah to know he cared. He had to stop worrying whether his actions or comments would make her shut down.

> Thanks. You, too.

This woman had him, heart and soul, and he didn't mind one bit.

CHAPTER 25

SARAH'S ALARM WOKE HER up earlier than she wanted. The clock in the shower read ten past five in the morning. By the time she dressed and found her way downstairs, she saw Brandon's truck pull into the driveway.

She had met him at the door, so the doorbell wouldn't wake everyone.

"Happy Thanksgiving, Sarah," Brandon handed her sparkling grape juice for dinner and she set it in the refrigerator.

Sarah locked eyes with Brandon. "You're here early."

"I couldn't stay away," his husky voice said, never breaking his intense gaze.

Her stomach fluttered with excitement. Thinking of Lily's nudge last night, Sarah pranced toward him. Gripping his shoulders, she pushed to the balls of her feet and pressed a chaste kiss to his lips.

"Who are you and what have you done with Sarah?" He said in a hushed tone.

She swallowed a giggle threatening to escape and playfully shoved his arm. The last thing she needed was her dad to say he told her so. Even though he did.

Gus's hoarse voice cleared behind her. "Great. You're here, so you'll help her with the turkey, right?" Gus asked Brandon.

"Happy Thanksgiving to you, too, Old Man."

"Yeah, yeah." Gus grumbled and returned up the stairs.

Sarah turned to Brandon. "Can you say he looked like himself?"

Brandon shrugged. "In his defense, it's quarter to six in the morning. Does anyone besides you look like their best self this early?"

"Aw. so sweet, but don't think that earned you too many brownie points; you're gutting the bird."

In the kitchen, she cut vegetables and placed them in dishes with lids, so she could place them back in the refrigerator until the parade. Thoughts of how domestic this felt ran through her mind. Why wasn't Brandon married? Would she ever consider getting married again? Doubtful.

Brandon tapped Sarah on the shoulder. "Earth to Sarah." He startled her, causing her to jump a foot off the floor and drop the knife. "I just need to know what to do with the turkey remains. Don't throw a knife at me," Brandon laughed as he backed away with his hands up.

"Sorry."

"Everything okay?"

She nodded and pointed her finger at him. "Don't think about getting me back."

"Okay. I will try this, though." Brandon grabbed a dish towel, twirled it, and whipped it at Sarah.

"Ow! Oh, you." Sarah swiped a towel off the counter and returned the whip, but Brandon caught the towel and pulled her close to him. He lifted Sarah up by the waist and planted a quick kiss on her lips.

He returned her to the floor, but held her gaze, running his fingers down her cheek, neck, and arms, sending a surging warmth through her body. He pulled her close, squeezing her ribs. She tilted her head to the side, anticipating his next move.

The air between them seemed to crackle, and the couple's lips met in a frenzy. Sarah gently placed her hands on Brandon's biceps and tried to pull him impossibly closer. She felt Brandon's thumbs near the sides of her chest, sending a rush of awareness through her body. Time seemed to stand still for Sarah when Brandon deepened the kiss, eliciting a moan from both of them.

Many minutes later, Brandon pulled his lips from hers, and moved her thick, blond hair from her shoulder with his nose. A trail of lingering kisses on her neck, right below her jaw bone, caused shivers to run down her spine. A wave of warmth and emotion hit her, causing her to pull back, her breath catching in her throat and her chest heaving.

He rested his forehead on hers, and she embraced the thrilling moment they had just shared. "I suppose we need to get dinner going if we're going to eat today."

Sounding disappointed, Brandon agreed. She dragged her hand from his shoulder across his chest before her hand fell to her side.

For the rest of the morning, the air in the kitchen buzzed with activity as they worked together, their hands sometimes brushing, the scent of freshly brewed coffee mingling with the aromas of cooking food.

By noontime, Jill, Jerry, and their kids arrived. Jenny and Joe disappeared with Lily to her room, while Josie colored with the markers and books Jill brought from home. Jill set a homemade apple pie on the counter. "Everyone makes pumpkin, and I like to be different," Jill explained.

Shortly after, Evelyn and Caleb knocked on the door. Brandon sighed. "It'll be alright." She gave him a side hug. He squeezed her tight, like he was trying to steal strength from her to deal with his dad.

Sarah watched her dad straighten his shirt and check his appearance in the hall mirror. She caught her dad's eye and gave him a smile. "Barbara will approve," she assured him.

"The snow is picking up out there." Caleb sat in the living room with Gus while Evelyn joined Brandon and Sarah in the kitchen.

She kissed her son's cheek. "Happy Thanksgiving, Son."

Brandon's tenderness with his mom struck Sarah. He is a man she could see herself with. Most likely.

"Sarah, I'd like you to meet my mom, Evelyn."

Sarah wiped her hands on a towel and extended her hand. "It's a pleasure to meet you."

"Oh, come here." Evelyn waved Sarah's hand away and pulled her in for a hug, surprising Sarah, yet making her feel warm inside.

Pulling back and focusing on her son, Evelyn smiled. "Why don't you head in with your dad and I'll get to know Sarah."

"Don't scare her away or tell her embarrassing stories."

"Aw, come on. That's what moms are supposed to do," Sarah pouted.

"I will ask Gus for some stories then."

"Nevermind." They laughed as Brandon kissed her cheek and let out a big breath before entering the living room.

Evelyn knew her way around a kitchen. Between the two of them, they had everything either done, cooking or waiting to be cooked when a spot on the stove cleared.

"Hi, Barbara, I'm glad you could make it." Sarah heard her dad greet the doctor. She and Evelyn joined everyone in the living.

"The roads are just getting a little slick, but other than that, it's beautiful out there." Sarah liked how positive Barbara was about everything.

Sarah noticed Caleb's body stiffened when she entered the room. His eyes darted her way when Brandon introduced them. Then he returned to his conversation with Jerry. As Brandon walked to his spot on the couch, he whispered something in his dad's ear. Caleb gave her a forced smile.

Don't put yourself out, Sarah thought, returning a pleasant smile.

Meanwhile, Caleb encouraged Jerry to pressure Brandon into expanding his business, which would mean Brandon taking out a substantial loan from the bank Jerry operated. Bolting from the couch, Brandon called over his shoulder, "Don't pay any attention to him Jerry, I'm doing just fine."

Sarah could hear the tension in Brandon's voice. She followed him into the kitchen and slid her hand over his back, and his muscles relaxed. He turned his head to meet Sarah's eyes and smiled. Then he leaned over and whispered, "I wish you and I alone. I have to keep praying for God to give me strength to control myself."

Sarah's stomach fluttered as he leaned in for a kiss, but their moment didn't last.

"Mom," Lily hollered down the stairs. "Kurt's dad burnt the turkey—"

Before Lily could ask for them to come over, Sarah interrupted, "Tell them to head over."

"Thanks, Mom," Lily replied.

"That's the exact opposite of what I just said," Brandon joked.

"We're not alone anyway," Sarah smirked.

Sarah set out all the serving trays with vegetables, dip, crackers, and cheese. She encouraged everyone to have a little something to eat while they waited for Kurt and his parents to arrive.

Next to Brandon's parents, Sarah felt underdressed in her full-length button up the front flowered dress. Evelyn wore a skirt suit to match Caleb's orange shirt and charcoal pant suit.

Brandon pressed his chest to her back and draped his arm over her shoulder, snatching a cucumber off the tray. "You look beautiful," he said, as if he could hear her thoughts. "Trying to impress my parents is impossible. I gave that up a long time ago. You've already won me, so do not worry about what anyone else, especially my parents, thinks."

Sarah was thankful for Brandon's sweet demeanor. It put her at ease.

Once Kurt and his parents, Cherie and Dan, arrived, everyone hurried into the dining room so they could eat.

As they sat down to dinner, Gus gave the blessing. "Dear Jesus, thank you so much for letting us gather together on this snowy day. We thank you so much for the abundance of food. Please help everyone get something good to eat today and help this food nourish our bodies, so we can do Your will. Help us to enjoy the food and each other's company. Please keep everyone safe as they travel today, amen."

Sarah asked Brandon to carve the turkey. That was something Jake always did.

"It would be an honor." They brushed hands as she passed him the knife.

Jill sighed, bringing everyone's attention to the moment. Fortunately, everyone focused more on piling food onto their plates than her.

Happy chatter filled the air. Lily and Kurt whispered at the table's far end while her dad and Barbara drew their chairs together, feigning more space for others.

After helping clean up, Barbara thanked Sarah for dinner. "I hate to eat and run, but I have to cover the ER tonight."

"Thanks for coming today. I really enjoyed having you here." Gus's nervous voice made Sarah laugh. "Let me walk you out."

As Gus reached the front door, the Jamieson clan bid him adieu. "Sorry Gus, we've got to get some sleep. Jerry and I are going shopping at midnight," Jill explained.

"Thank you so much for having us over. We appreciate everything." Jerry shook Gus's hand.

"No problem. I really enjoyed having you guys over. Come back any-time." Gus slapped Jerry on the back.

Sarah noticed that Jerry didn't fall as forward as he usually did when Gus slapped him like that.

Gus didn't look so good. He was gray faced and weak. "Are you okay, Dad?"

"I'm just tired. I'll get some rest tonight," Gus assured her with a big smile.

Sarah asked, "Why are you so happy?"

"I have a dinner date with Barbara," He cooed, puffing out his chest.

"Alright, Old Man." Brandon slapped Gus on the shoulder.

Kurt's parents asked to take Lily ice skating. "It's an annual tradition. We go to the ice rink after our turkey dinner," Cherie explained.

Once Sarah agreed, they were gone. That only left Brandon's parents. She heard a lively discussion taking place in the other room.

"For the umpteenth time, Dad, I am working as hard as I can. I look into hiring an apprentice after the holidays. I am not taking out a loan for advertising. Word of mouth is working just fine."

"Sorry to interrupt," Sarah shyly stated. "Does anyone want pie?"

"No thank you, Sarah, Caleb and I must get going. Dinner was excellent. Thank you for your hospitality." Brandon's dad stood up, still glaring at his son. "We'll finish this conversation later," Caleb informed his son. Both Caleb and Evelyn quickly put on their jackets and left.

"Well, that was awkward," Sarah said, trying to lighten the mood. Brandon half smiled at her. Sarah wondered if she had overstepped some unspoken boundary by calling attention to the tension in the room.

"Listen here Brandon, you are the best contractor in southern Maine. You know that and your dad knows that," Gus said, trying to assure him. He wants what every father does for his children—success. Gus patted Brandon's shoulder. "I'm heading to my store for a bit, unless you need me."

With that, the loud roar of laughter and chaos hours ago ceased and one could hear a pin drop. Brandon stood up from the table and Sarah cried, "Are you leaving too?"

"Not if you don't want me to," Brandon replied.

Sarah pushed in the dining room chairs and turned out the lights before heading into the living room. "I thought we could relax and talk for a bit."

Sitting on the couch sideways to face Sarah, Brandon rested his arm on the back of the couch. "Thank you so much for dinner. Everything turned out excellent."

"With your help. Thanksgiving would have been very different for everyone without that turkey, so thank you."

Brandon excused himself to the restroom.

"I'm going to check on Dad, I'll be right back." Sarah hollered.

As she approached the side door of the store, it was wide open. For her dad, that was odd, so she ran to the store.

"Dad, where are you?" Sarah called when she didn't see her dad in the kitchen or at the front end of the store. Sarah checked in the greenhouse, but couldn't find him anywhere. Getting more anxious, Sarah ran back to the store and yelled louder, "Dad, this isn't funny. Come out here now."

Just then, she saw Brandon walking toward the store. "I can't find my dad. He's not in the greenhouse or the store." The panic filled Sarah's body, becoming ever present in her voice.

Each crunching footstep on the slick snow sent a jolt of icy fear through Sarah as she hurried around the house. Her thoughts lingered on the image of her father's tired face, a heavy weight of concern settling in her chest. "I never should have waited this long to check on him," Sarah verbally beat herself up aloud.

Meanwhile, Sarah heard Brandon yell, "Gus, what happened?"

Sarah watched Brandon rush to Gus's side and turned him over. His legs were dangling off the porch steps.

"Sarah quick, call 9-1-1. Tell them he's unconscious and his face is white as a ghost, with streaks of blue forming around his lips," Brandon yelled before starting CPR.

Sarah dashed around the corner and skipped three porch steps to enter the house. The dispatcher assured Sarah help was on the way. It seemed like an eternity before the ambulance arrived. Brandon directed Sarah to go with her dad and he would wait for Lily. Without hesitation, Sarah hopped in the front of the ambulance as it sped out of the driveway.

Chapter 26

At the emergency room, doctors assisted the paramedics with the gurney as they raced down the hall. Sarah overheard one paramedic say he lost him on the way in for about two minutes. The thought of living without her dad, too, crushed her.

Sarah stopped outside the swinging doors that read, Authorized Personnel Only. Within a few minutes, she watched the paramedics exit. They assured Sarah that her dad was in good hands with the doctors, but couldn't answer any of the zillion questions she had running through her head.

"Did Dad always have health issues, and he just kept them from me?" Sarah wondered aloud. If she hadn't been so preoccupied with Brandon, she probably would have heard Dad fall, or she would have thought to check on him sooner. Sarah blamed herself.

She paced the floor in the emergency room. After three and a half hours of waiting, Sarah started getting angry that doctors were keeping her in the dark. If they had to do surgery, didn't they need her permission before they did anything? What if they were still trying to revive him? That made little sense.

The sight of Pastor Pete put Sarah at ease. She told him in one big breath what happened, and then he prayed with her. "Dear Lord, please guide the doctors' and nurses' hands to help heal Gus. Thank you for putting Brandon in Sarah's life to help her get through this season of her life. Lord, please be with Sarah and help her be at peace, no matter what happens. It's your will, Lord, that we embrace. Your will because you know best! Thank you for being such a kind and faithful God, amen."

When Sarah opened her eyes, she noticed that a young doctor who looked a few years older than Lily was finally approaching them, carrying a patient's chart in a metal covering. He was wearing a long white medical jacket and blue scrub pants. The first thing he let her know was that her dad had had a massive heart attack and needed immediate triple by-pass surgery in order for him to have a chance at survival. Sarah stared at the doctor with her hand covering her gaping mouth. Unable to ask any of those burning questions, she stared at the doctor, who could apparently read Sarah's mind.

"Your dad is fine now and is being transferred to Intensive Care. He is lucky you found him when you did." Sarah cringed at his last comment. The thought that her focus on Brandon could have cost her dad's life made her ill.

"See, you found him in time—you have nothing to regret." It was like Pastor Pete could read her mind and knew she blamed herself.

"A nurse will be here to bring you to his room. Do you have any questions for me?" The doctor asked Sarah.

"Do you know what caused this, Doctor..." Sarah searched for a name tag, but couldn't find one on his coat.

"I'm sorry; Dr. Philbrook." He extended his hand to Sarah. "From the plaque buildup on his arteries, I'd say years of unhealthy eating, extreme amounts of stress, and a lack of exercise initiated the heart attack."

"Thank you, doctor." As the man walked away, a bubbly blonde, pencil thin nurse came to escort Sarah to Gus's room on the seventh floor.

Pastor Pete told Sarah he'd be back tomorrow to see Gus. Sarah thanked him for coming. It clicked in her mind, a sudden understanding illuminating her face. Brandon must have called him.

"Hi, my name is Michelle. I'll be your dad's nurse this evening. If you need anything, please let me know."

Sarah turned to the woman. "Is he awake yet?"

"He might be awake by the time we get back," Michelle explained, "but he'll likely be groggy, disoriented, and a little confused about his surroundings."

When they reached Gus's room, he was still sleeping, so the nurse brought Sarah a cot and then left to do her rounds.

Sarah called Brandon. "Dad's okay."

"That's great."

"Did Lily get home yet?" Sarah could hear the hostility in her voice as she talked with Brandon.

"She's upstairs changing. She'd like to see Gus. What do you want me to do?"

Sarah agreed to let Lily come in and thanked Brandon for bringing her and then hung up. She slipped her phone back in her pocket and sat beside her dad, crying as she took in the sight. He had an IV for hydration, a breathing tube, and patches of hair removed from his chest.

Discouraged, Sarah squeezed her dad's hand. "Thank you, Lord, for watching over him," Sarah said aloud.

"Mom," Lily ran into Gus's room and wrapped her arms around Sarah. Though Lily wasn't crying, her mom knew she had been.

"Grandpa is going to be fine. He had a massive heart attack, so the doctors had to perform triple-bypass surgery to help blood flow to his heart," Sarah explained.

Looking up, when Brandon entered the room, Sarah said, "Thank you for bringing Lily here." Before she could tell him he was free to head out, Brandon interrupted her, almost as if he could read her mind.

"Any time. I'd do anything for all of you."

Lily released the hold she had on her mom. Looking first at Brandon, then Sarah, she asked, "Mom, can I have some time with Grandpa by myself?"

Looking confused and anxious, Sarah replied, "Sure, honey, I'll be right outside the door if you need me."

Brandon stepped aside to let Sarah pass first. He placed his hand on the small of her back to lead her out into the hall, but Sarah flinched at his touch. She dreaded what was to come.

CHAPTER 27

BRANDON PULLED SARAH'S TENSE body into his and hugged her hard, though she never uncrossed her arms. "I'm glad your dad is going to be okay."

"No thanks to me," Sarah blurted out angrily. "I should have paid more attention to how long he'd been gone. He could have died while I was talking with you," she added.

Moving Sarah away from his body, still holding onto her shoulders, he said, "You can't blame yourself. *Or me,* he wanted to add, but didn't. "What happened to your dad was God's will."

Brandon's voice, tight with barely controlled frustration, betrayed his anxiety; a sickening premonition told him his budding romance with Sarah was about to end too soon.

Sarah stepped back and Brandon's arms fell to his sides in defeat. She avoided his gaze. "I need to spend all of my time helping Dad recover, so there won't be any time for anything or anyone else."

Slowly shaking his head in frustration, Brandon lifted Sarah's chin and stared directly into her eyes. "I know you have feelings for me. Our kisses, hugs, and talks tell me all I need to know. You can try to push me away now to punish yourself, but you'll never hide your feelings from God and if He wants us to be together, we will be."

Tears pooled in Sarah's eyes as she gazed at him. "I will give you whatever space you think you need. Just know, I love you and I am here for you." Brandon kissed Sarah on the cheek. Before he walked away, he whispered in her ear, "You'll never be happy until Christ is first in your life and you trust my feelings for you." He kissed her on the cheek again and walked away.

Two agonizing weeks later, Brandon waited in his truck at Gus's. Finally, Barbara pulled into the driveway and Brandon pushed open his door, hopped out of his truck, and leaned against the hood, waiting for her to park.

Lily exited first, sprinting toward Brandon into his arms. "My grandpa is home. Thanks for being there for us."

"That's great, Lily. I told you I'll always be there for you." Brandon released his hold on Lily and she ran to open the house door.

As Brandon opened Sarah's door and helped her out, he asked, "What do I have to do to get you to run into my arms like Lily did?" When Sarah didn't respond, Brandon stuffed his hands in his jean pockets. "I'm sorry. All night I've been praying for your dad, Lily, you..." *and us.* He kept that last part to himself.

Sarah smiled at Brandon and placed her palm on his chest. "Thanks. I thought a lot about our conversation, too. If you have some time, we could talk now. Well, after I clean up," she clarified.

"Okay. You go clean up and I'll help Gus inside."

Thirty minutes later, Brandon's attention pulled as Sarah descended the stairs in a blue, long-sleeved, v-neck sweater with her alma mater logo on the front and a pair of lounge pants. Her beauty radiated.

"I'm going to call Kurt." Lily ran upstairs.

"Your dad is resting in the room down here. The doctor said he showed improvement faster than any of his other patients." Brandon held out his hand for Sarah to sit with him.

She lowered herself next to Brandon on the couch. "Yeah. My dad has a will to live." She rubbed her palms over her face. "I am so sorry that I blamed you for what happened to my dad. I know we were powerless, but I feared for my dad. If I'm being completely honest, I'm still struggling with our relationship, and it was an easy way out."

"Sarah, you have nothing to be sorry for. Everyone reacts to a crisis in their own way. You are still going through the grieving process and you're trying to raise Lily. Give yourself a break."

"There are twelve days until Christmas." Sarah fell back against the back of the couch and let out an enormous sigh, looking the most stressed he'd ever seen her.

Brandon pulled Sarah onto his chest with his powerful arms. "You can lean on me."

She ignored him and said, "Barbara has taken a leave from the hospital. She's going to move into the spare bedroom and watch over Gus here."

"Interesting. That is going above and beyond the Hippocratic Oath," Brandon chortled, knowing Gus's feelings for Barbara. Maybe she reciprocated them.

Sarah tensed against him. Was she concerned about her dad moving on, or did her discomfort come from their blooming relationship? He needed to make his intentions clear. With a boldness not of his own, Brandon pulled her back, so she leaned against his arm. Her groggy eyes, threatening to close. "The last two weeks, I've felt like I was climbing a mountain and not making any gain in elevation, yet losing oxygen just the same. Meeting you showed me I want more than just work. Until I met you, working all the time didn't bother me." He kissed her forehead. "But now my life feels hollow without you. I love you, Sarah."

He felt her inhale.

Only the sizzling sound of electricity pounded in his ears. If this was unrequited love, he'd have to figure a way to move on, but he didn't believe that was the case. He saw affection in Sarah's eyes when she looked at him. The intensity of her kisses, and tender feeling of her touch. She may not know it or be willing to admit it yet, but she loved him. All he could do was sit, the anticipation a tight knot in his stomach, and wait.

CHAPTER 28

GUS GOT VERY CRANKY doing nothing. Sarah watched her dad spend most of his time walking around the house, building up his stamina or reading a book because he got bored with television very quickly. Even more she admired Barbara as she worked with the patience of Job alongside Gus, trusting that God would transform him and change his heart back to the Gus they knew and admired.

Brandon's presence at the house the week before Christmas didn't translate into Sarah seeing him more, as he was busy installing the new shower and toilet bar for Gus's convenience. The most she saw him was when he hung the store sign and at night when he gave her a kiss before leaving.

Sarah was very uneasy about Brandon's behavior. He went from being all over her to avoiding her this week. What happened? He seemed jittery around her. Sarah wasn't sure what she'd done or said to cause this. A knot of anxiety tightened in her chest. Finally, Friday night came and Sarah packed her last order. Brandon entered the store looking as wiped as her. "Hey, are you done for the night?" Sarah asked, wondering if he'd ask to spend time with her.

"I am. A hot shower and my bed is what this man needs."

Sarah's face saddened when she realized Brandon was leaving. "Will I see you tomorrow?"

Brandon stumbled on his words a bit, "I... Tomorrow I'm... I have to pick up something and have it ready for church on Sunday, so I can't get together tomorrow, but I'll definitely see you on Sunday."

Before Sarah could protest, Brandon gave her a warm hug and a tender kiss. Though the kiss lingered, she knew something was up, but she couldn't put her finger on it.

Given that many people went to church on Christmas Sunday, Barbara drove Sarah, Gus, and Lily to church early. Lily sat with Kurt, while Gus slid into a pew with Barbara.

Sarah looked around the sanctuary for Brandon. Instead, Miss Clancy rushed over to give her a hug. Sarah loved Miss Clancy. Her bright spirit and cheerful demeanor stood out like a beacon of hope.

"Where's Brandon?" Miss Clancy could barely contain herself. She was grinning like the Cheshire cat.

"I'm not sure. I haven't seen him." Sarah thought this was odd because Miss Clancy never asked her his whereabouts before. "Do you know something I don't?" Sarah asked playfully, but she expected an answer.

Miss Clancy shrugged her shoulders and excused herself. "The little kids are waiting for their candy. See you later."

Just then, Brandon came up behind Sarah. He was sweating more than he did working in the warm September sun. Sarah pulled at the front of her shirt. Maybe it was a little hot in here.

She laced their fingers together. "You look handsome in this tie. She fingered the silky material."

"Thanks."

"I never expected to see you in anything besides jeans and a T-shirt, or just jeans on a hot day." She flirted.

He let out a distracted chuckle.

"Are you okay? You don't look well." His outfit had taken Sarah by surprise that she didn't notice his pale complexion.

"I feel like I might throw up, but I know what it's from; I'll be fine." Brandon led Sarah into a pew near the front.

As Sarah passed the pew where her dad and Barbara were sitting, Gus reached out and grabbed her hand. "Remember, dear, it's all about God's plan. We just need to be obedient."

"Okaaaaay."

Pastor Pete took his place behind the pulpit. "We have a special this morning, but before we get to that, the Holy Spirit has prompted me to start with something else." He gave Brandon an assured look.

What was that all about?

"Healing is a part of life," Pastor Pete began. "Whether physical, mental, or spiritual, all healing happens through our relationship with God."

Eureka! How did he know she needed to hear this? She must have made some facial expression because Brandon leaned over and asked her if she was okay. Without taking her eyes off Pastor Pete, she nodded.

After reading First Corinthians 10:13, the pastor said, "If anyone needs to let go of the junk they have inside in order to let God heal them, now is the time."

Sarah felt paralyzed. Her brain was telling her to move, but her legs were as heavy as cement blocks. God, is that you? "What do I need to let go of? Are you telling me to go up to the altar? What am I supposed to say?" Questions swirled around Sarah's head.

Pastor Pete interrupted her thoughts. "For those of you seeking a rela-tionship with God, all you have to do is ask Him to forgive you of your sins and that starts the relationship."

Sarah laughed when Pastor Pete answered the question she intended for God. She watched a few people leave their seats and kneel at the altar.

Sarah brushed Brandon's arm and excused herself by him and went to the altar. Sarah caught Pastor Pete's eye, and he gave her a big reassuring smile, as if he was talking to her the whole time. Did he know she needed to reestablish her relationship with God? How could he? The realization hit her only moments ago.

He knelt down with Sarah, cupped her hands, and asked her if she wanted to rededicate her life to Jesus.

Her eyes brimmed with unshed tears as Sarah looked the pastor in the face. "Yes."

Pastor prayed the sinner's prayer with her, but he didn't stop there. "Romans 10: 9-10 says, 'If you confess with your mouth, Jesus is Lord, and believe in your heart that God raised him from the dead, you will be saved. For it is with your heart that you believe and are justified, and it is with your mouth that you confess and are saved.' Do you believe this, Sarah?"

Sarah shook her head, unable to even speak. She had continuously wiped her never ending tears with her sleeve. At that moment, Sarah felt the embrace of her daughter. Sarah could never mistake her daughter's touch.

"Sarah, now I want you to pray. Let God hear how you are feeling." Pastor Pete placed his hand on her shoulder.

"God, I am so sorry for being a sinner; please forgive me. I believe that you gave up your son, Jesus Christ, for me. Jesus, I know that you shed your blood and died for me, and I want to repay you by living and obeying your word. I declare here and now to abandon intentional sin. Striving instead to bring glory and honor to your name through obedience. Lord, please forgive me for my sins and let me honor you. Show me your will for me, so I can make you proud, amen."

Sarah wiped her eyes as she lifted her head. Sarah embraced Lily, who was holding her hand and smiling at her. Then Sarah noticed Brandon, Jill, and Jerry standing behind her and behind them were more of the parishioners. "Thank you, everyone."

While people hugged Sarah and found their seats again, she felt the weight of the world lifted off her shoulders. Her worry lessened, and Sarah felt free to live.

Chapter 29

Pastor Pete made his way back to the pulpit. "We can always celebrate our Savior's birth, but today is Christmas Sunday and there is no better time to worship Jesus," Pastor Pete began. "Miss Pearle's Sunday School kiddos want to show you what this day looked like so many years ago." Then he invited the nine kids to join him on stage and they acted out a skit reflecting Jesus' birth. Brandon placed his arm around Sarah's shoulders and pulled her closer to him. As the third Magi presented Jesus with Frankincense, Brandon excused himself to the bathroom.

He returned when the angels entered full of spirit, and in unison said, "Glory to God in the Highest and on Earth, peace to men!"

Pastor Pete stood and returned to the pulpit, waiting for the crowd to finish their applause. "How about those kids? Great little witnesses for the troubled souls in the world surrounding us. God always gives us surprises, how many have you missed?" Pastor Pete asked rhetorically and continued, "Micah 5:2 tells us that King Herod's men knew Christ would be born in Bethlehem, but they didn't recognize Him when he entered the world." The pastor took a sip of water before he continued. "The Jews expected some fireworks, a red carpet and a band to reveal the Messiah who would save them from the Romans, but they missed the little baby lying in the manger. This simple sign of God's love is still a shock to people today. It's not surprising to me that the world missed God's surprise in Jesus because it's only faith that makes Christ visible. God brought Jesus into this world to give us salvation because we could not save ourselves. Had he not been born, he couldn't have died for our sins and rose from the grave. God bestowed an unexpected human baby upon us in a barn—our only recourse."

Continuing, with his attention focused on Sarah, he said, "God is full of surprises. He does what He wants and doesn't ask for our counsel, even when we beg and plead for Him to listen. He surprises us with His next moves because we walk along with him in faith, not knowing what He will do next. We; however, thanks to the Holy Spirit, can do as God directs when His ways make no sense at all. We just trust that the Holy Spirit guides us to do God's will. Our job is to obey His word and work hard not to miss one of the many surprises He puts in our lives."

Just then, Pastor Pete motioned Brandon to join him on stage. Confusion and nerves filled Sarah as she scanned the sanctuary. From across the room, Miss Clancy smiled and waved at her.

Brandon took Pastor Pete's place behind the pulpit, thanking him for the introduction. He first apologized to the congregation for taking a little extra time this week. "I promise I won't take as long as Pastor Pete did to preach." Brandon shot a joking look at his buddy as the crowd laughed.

"Get on with it," Pastor chortled into his headset microphone.

Even though Pastor Pete and Brandon were friends, Sarah thought Brandon's joke telling was a bit out of place. Why did Brandon look so nervous? He spoke in front of the congregation all the time?

"As you all know, Christmas is almost here, and it is a very special time of year," Brandon began. "It's a time to remember how we should act year round—focusing on God's love and our obedience to Him. I like to think of myself as an obedient person to God and for the past month or so, He has told me to be patient and understanding and He would give me the desires of my heart." Brandon started pacing. Then he left the stage and made his way down the center aisle toward Sarah. He stopped in front of her. She wasn't sure what her expression was, but a baffled feeling washed over her. She saw Miss Clancy across the aisle, still smiling at her.

"Sarah, I've grown to love you and now I know you love me, too. God has given me the answer to my prayers—He's given me you. I want to spend the rest of my life with you and show you how much I love you. When I look at you and Lily, I see my future." As Brandon dropped to one knee, he pulled out a red velvet ring box, took Sarah's hand, and asked, "Will you please give me the greatest earthly gift of becoming my wife?"

Dumbfounded, Sarah couldn't speak. Her eyes filled with tears. She looked for Lily and her facial expression asked for her daughter's approval. Lily nodded and smiled gleefully at her mother. Turning to Brandon, "Yes, of course, I'll marry you!" Brandon put the ring on Sarah's finger and embraced her with such excitement that he lifted her off the floor. As the congregation cheered, Sarah looked at Miss Clancy again, who winked at her. She knew the whole time!

After Pastor Pete closed the congregation in prayer, Lily rushed over to her mom. "I knew! Brandon asked Grandpa and I last week if he could ask you."

Sarah hugged Brandon with one arm, thanking him for his respect. "So, is this why you were acting so weird?"

"Of course." Brandon leaned over and whispered in her ear, "Plus, I'm losing self control around you." He smirked and shrugged. "I'm hoping you don't mind a short engagement."

Miss Clancy hugged Sarah and offered congratulations. "You know everything, don't you, Miss Clancy?"

"She's got a way of making people talk," Brandon snickered.

Jerry and Pastor Pete slapped Brandon on the back and gave him a manly handshake with a one-armed hug.

"Just friends, huh?" Jill hugged Sarah. "I knew you two were good for each other."

Jill gathered her family and headed out to drop one of her children off at a Christmas party. "Sorry to run, but we have to get somewhere on time today."

"That will never happen," Jerry called as he pushed his way to Sarah and congratulated her with a quick hug.

"Merry Christmas guys, I'll see you later." Sarah waved bye to the entire Jamieson gang.

At home, the dinner Gus and Barbara prepared was ready for everyone to eat.

Brandon asked Gus for his daughter's hand in marriage about a week ago, so Gus anticipated a big dinner to celebrate the occasion.

"You knew, too, Dad?"

"Of course he did," Brandon interrupted. "You don't think I'd ask you before I asked him if it was okay, do you?"

Sarah smiled. "I suppose not."

On his drive home from church, Brandon called his mom to share that Sarah said yes to his proposal. Evelyn offered her well wishes but couldn't join him for lunch as she and Caleb had other plans. Brandon mentioned he thought this was his dad's way of expressing his disdain for his son getting married. Sarah's heart wept for him. Though he said nothing, she could tell that his family's absence bothered him.

After cleaning up, Brandon left, saying he had to run an errand. Gus fell asleep on the couch and Lily and Kurt were in the office downloading music. Sarah sat down at the kitchen table with Barbara, who played solitaire faster than anyone she had ever seen. "Is it really fun going that fast?" Sarah started the conversation.

Barbara laughed, but stayed laser-focused on her hand. "Yeah. I used to compete in a solitaire exhibition. The fastest time won."

"You must have won a lot," Sarah stated, based on Barbara's speediness.

"I held my own," Barbara replied. "There we go, last card. That was a tough hand. Do you play cards?" Barbara asked Sarah.

Sarah smiled and nodded, hoping Barbara would ask her to play something before Brandon returned. "My favorite is gin," Sarah added confidently.

While Barbara dealt the cards, Sarah said, "Thank you so much for overseeing my dad's care. Without you, he would have been in the hospital longer and his spirits would have been shot. You are great with him. He's not an easy patient." Sarah acknowledged.

Barbara, with a loving smile, accepted Sarah's compliment and with a quick raise of her eyebrows that showed she agreed. "Gus is all about being mobile, so it is difficult for him to slow down," Barbara defended him. "But God has ways of forcing us to obey His will and since your dad doesn't listen that well sometimes to people on Earth, God helped him out."

"Sometimes?" Sarah questioned with a chuckle. "How about all the time?" She added as she organized the hand that Barbara dealt her.

"Touché. He has a difficult time listening all the time, so God slowed him down," Barbara finished.

Within four turns, Barbara declared victory. "Gin!"

"What?" Sarah exclaimed. "You really are a master card player, huh?" She added in defeat and fanned her cards on the table, revealing only two matches.

Barbara gathered the cards into a pile. "Sarah, I don't want you to think I'm trying to replace your mother. Gus worried I wanted to get married and if I didn't, he thought that meant I wouldn't come around. That's not the case. I care for your dad very much, but my concern is with him getting better. Anything else will come if God wills it."

Sarah appreciated the doctor's words. "You're good for him in any role you both decide."

Gus woke at the same time Brandon returned. Sarah greeted him with a kiss. "What's the surprise?" she asked, like a little kid at Christmas.

"Go look, it's in my truck," Brandon offered. He urged Lily to go with her mom because it involved her too.

"You got us a tree? Thank you so much." Sarah and Lily hugged him.

As soon as she released him, Lily ran toward the house. Thrashing through the front door, she hollered to Gus and Barbara, "Brandon got us a tree! We're putting it up right now."

CHAPTER 30

SARAH TUCKED LILY INTO bed when everyone left. Even though Lily said she was too big for this evening ritual, she loved talking with her mom before going to sleep, and Sarah knew that.

"Everything okay with you, Lil?" Sarah inquired.

"Fine, Mom, why?" Lily answered.

"You looked a little distant at dinner," Sarah explained.

"I'm fine. I guess the idea that I have to have Christmas Eve without Dad in a few days is sad."

"Me too, honey. Are you okay with the plan we just made?"

Lily's silence answered Sarah's question, but Lily tried to be understanding, "I'm fine with it, Mom."

Sarah didn't want to nag her daughter; that was a sure way to get a teenager to clam up, but she felt helpless. "Honey, you come first. If you're not okay with this, you need to tell me," Sarah persisted.

Lily explained to her that she got wrapped up in the excitement of the engagement. She knew that Brandon clearly loved her mom, and it reminded Lily of how her dad treated Sarah. But realizing that her dad was gone had just hit her and made her feel sad and guilty.

"You have nothing to feel guilty about, Lily," Sarah assured her daughter as she pulled her daughter close to her and rested her daughter's head on her chest and stroked Lily's beautiful hair.

"But I do. First, I let Dad down because I should have told Brandon that I didn't want him to ask you to marry him. But now that he has, I feel guilty about telling you this because I don't want you to be sad. Plus, I like Brandon. He's a good teacher, and he answers all my questions, so I don't want him mad at me either. But this is my first Christmas without my dad. Some people have their first holidays soon after the death of a loved one, so the pain is still new, but I've had all these months to heal and now the holidays come and I'm a mess again."

"So you don't want me to marry Brandon?" Sarah clarified.

"I don't know what I want," Lily said, dismayed.

"Well, no need to worry about it now. Let's get some rest. We have a lot of preparations before Christmas." Sarah kissed the top of her daughter's head, pulled up her covers and turned out her lights.

Christmas Eve morning, Sarah woke up more exhausted than when she went to bed. Sarah tossed and turned all night until she finally asked God to clear her mind and heart and give her the sleep she needed.

Sarah found Lily making marshmallow treats and peanut butter balls when she entered the kitchen. "Good morning, Mom!" Lily exclaimed. "Barbara took Grandpa for a walk to the end of the road. She said she'd call if you needed to go get them," she added as she put the dirty dishes in the sink to soak.

Sarah washed her hands and started gathering the mini hot dogs and the ingredients she needed to make them when Lily chirped, "Oh yeah, Brandon called. He'll be here at six o'clock."

"I'm confused," Sarah began, shaking her head. "I thought you wanted me to tell Brandon that plans changed."

"Things happen for a reason, Mom. I know I miss dad, just like you do, but I also know that Brandon loves you and I'm sure God will reveal a lot to me through this. That's what Kurt tells me, anyway."

Sarah closed her eyes and prayed silently before she put all the ingredients in the slow cooker.

Gus and Barbara returned from their walk. Sarah had noticed that her dad seemed out of breath.

"How did it go?" Sarah asked, focusing her attention on her dad.

"Slow!" Gus said in a discouraging tone.

"As expected, but very consistent," Barbara added as she assisted Gus to the sofa, where he had laid his feet on the ottoman and leaned back against the sofa cushions. "The cold air makes it more difficult, but from a medical standpoint, he is recovering well."

Sarah spent the rest of the morning preparing food. By the afternoon, Sarah wanted a nap, but instead she settled for a hot shower and the Christmas Eve service. Gus invited Brandon to join them since his parents didn't attend church. Besides, Gus already referred to Brandon as his son, so it seemed fitting. He also invited Barbara since her son was defending our country overseas and he knew that Barbara missed him dearly.

As the five of them walked into the church, Lily held the door for Gus and Barbara. Then Brandon held the door for Lily to enter the church. Putting his arm around Sarah's waist to have her enter, he whispered in her ear, "Are you okay?"

Sarah cringed, feeling dread seep into her bloodstream. She whispered, "We'll talk later."

They were early, so once they set their coats in the pew, Brandon took Sarah to his classroom. "What's wrong?" His concerned tone filled Sarah with more guilt as he sat next to her on the couch.

Sarah told him about the conversations she had with Lily.

Brandon held tight onto Sarah's hand the entire time. "What do you want to do?"

"What God wants me to do!" Sarah said without thinking. "Will you pray for us right now, please?" Sarah requested.

Instantly, Brandon clasped both of Sarah's hands together with his, shut his eyes, and began, "Lord, thank you for putting Sarah in my life. I know you are lending her to me for a reason. Please give me the opportunity to treat her the way you want me to, which is what she deserves. Lord, I pray you give Lily the understanding she needs to help her see that Sarah and I belong together. This type of understanding is way beyond her years, but Lord, I believe you can give it to her. I pray for Sarah. Lord, give her the strength to follow Your path. Instruct her to follow the Holy Spirit within her and do your will. Open her ears and heart, Lord, as she feels like she can't hear you, though based on what she told me and the words you gave her last night, I think she has her answer. Please don't let the enemy instill fear in her. Lord, we love you..."

Sarah peeked at Brandon while he was praying and noticed a smile emerge on his handsome face. She thanked God for putting him in her life; but at the same time she asked God to help her be the best mom and support Lily.

Sarah missed some of Brandon's prayer, but refocused her thoughts on his words when he asked the Lord to give him the strength and wisdom to wait as long as the Lord needed him to, so he could live the rest of his life with Sarah. "But Lord, I also release self to you right now, just like Jesus did in the Garden of Gethsemane. Even though I want to live my life with Sarah and Lily, Lord, I pray that Your will be done. Show me how to obey you, Lord. And convict us both so much that we cannot question Your will. In Jesus' name, amen."

"Mom, Brandon..." Lily shouted down the hall.

"We're in my classroom," Brandon called.

Poking her head in the room, Lily informed the couple that Pastor Pete was waiting for them.

Grabbing Sarah's hand, Brandon helped her off the couch. "Let's go, my love."

Lily grabbed her mom's other hand. As they walked down the hall, Lily rested her head on her mom's shoulder. Then she surprised her mom with a kiss on the cheek and three words she needed to hear from her daughter, "I love you."

When everyone arrived home, ease fell on Sarah as she got the food out and set them on trays.

Gus said grace and then the family enjoyed fantastic food and a present. Sarah learned more about Barbara's son, Matthew, and Pastor Pete's daughter, Melanie, who were engaged to be married. Matthew got orders to be in Afghanistan for three years and Melanie lived in Boston, where she was a sophomore at Boston College. Matthew was expected back when Melanie graduated with her bachelor's degree in social work, so the couple planned on getting married then.

Sarah enjoyed her conversation with Barbara because knowing these things made her existence more real. Also, Sarah could tell it pleased her dad when Sarah took an interest in getting to know Barbara.

"Lily, where's that boyfriend of yours?" Barbara inquired.

"He's in New York." Lily sounded dismal. "His family goes there from Christmas Eve through the New Year," Lily added.

After opening one present, Sarah shooed everyone off to bed so she could clean up and prepare the house. Sarah still didn't know what to do about Brandon, but then Lily returned to the room. "Good night Mom." She gave her mom a big hug. "Night, Brandon. See you two first thing in the morning. Beware Brandon, I wake up early on Christmas," Lily finished with a serious but playful tone.

"Sleep well, Lily, see you tomorrow morning," Brandon replied with a chuckle as she ran up the stairs.

"I guess that means I can stay," Brandon joked with Sarah.

"I guess so," Sarah replied with a half-hearted smile. She escorted Brandon to his room and gave him a hug and kiss goodnight.

Christmas morning, Brandon woke to the smell of waffles, eggs, and bacon. Stepping into the kitchen, he stared at his soon to be wife in amazement. How did she prepare all of this without burning something? Brandon wondered as he watched her put together another great meal.

Brandon walked up behind Sarah and gave her a hug. He wanted to hold on longer, but Sarah only paused for a brief moment. He knew she was focused on getting breakfast finished.

"Is this what I have to look forward to in marriage?" Brandon asked with excitement.

"Not at all," Sarah replied with a laugh. "I'd expect you to be helping me with a meal like this," Sarah added.

"Well, not at all the answer I wanted, but at least you're honest," Brandon smiled.

She strutted over to him, spatula in hand and gave him a hug. "I'm sorry. Merry Christmas. I'll cook like this as long as you do the bacon—it's disgusting," Sarah finished.

Laughing, Brandon gave Sarah another hug. "Deal. He grabbed the package from the refrigerator and started cooking it in the microwave.

After breakfast, Lily begged to open presents. He'd told Sarah about a tradition at his house and was pleased when she incorporated it today.

"We have to remember what today really means. Jesus was born today. With that said, let's read a Bible story before we get lost in our day."

Sarah opened her Bible to Luke chapter two and read until she wept like a baby. She handed her Bible to Brandon, and he finished the story. "And suddenly there was with the angel a multitude of the heavenly host praising God, and saying, Glory to God in the highest, and on earth peace, good will toward men."

Christmas Day came and went. Everyone exchanged gifts and then enjoyed their new items. They shared a plentiful Christmas lunch and then returned to their new presents. At dinner time Brandon, Sarah, and Lily went to the soup kitchen to serve food to the homeless, while Barbara and Gus stayed home playing cards. Sarah hoped that this experience would show Lily how lucky she was to have a family, all her possessions, and overall a good life. The sight of those really in need can help people realize things they never entertained before.

Brandon watched Lily scoop potatoes for two hundred fifty individuals during their shift. He grew concerned with Sarah's quietness. Though Brandon wanted to know the details of her thoughts, he let her be. He hoped she'd talk to him soon.

As the trio left the soup kitchen, they made plans to volunteer again on New Year's Eve.

Though he'd spent every day since Christmas with Sarah, Brandon felt a wall between them. He placed his hand on Sarah's shoulder and whispered in her ear. "Are you okay?"

She continued to serve food as she replied, "Yeah, just trying to hear the Lord."

A pit formed in his stomach and he feared the worst. The one instance when he wanted time to slow down, it seemed like the hands on the clock were circling in warp speed and before Brandon knew it, they were closing the kitchen.

They returned to Sarah's just before midnight. Lily thanked Brandon for the ride, crawled out of his truck, and dragged herself to the door.

"Ready to watch the ball drop, Lil?" Gus asked, opening it for her.

"Yeah right. I'm going to bed."

"I'll be in shortly, Dad," Sarah hollered as he shut the door.

"Want to sit on the porch?" Brandon asked, as he placed his hand on her lower back.

"Sounds good." Her flat tone made Brandon more nervous.

"I can't believe it's almost a new year," Brandon started with small talk.

"Fifteen seconds," Sarah clarified.

"We're going to be okay, right?" Brandon questioned.

Sarah hesitated momentarily. "I always told you that Lily comes first. While I'd die for her, Jesus comes first in my life now and that makes me a better person overall." Sarah paused briefly before continuing.

Brandon nodded, happy that Sarah rededicated her life to Jesus. But a cold dread seeped into his gut. His palms sweat and his stomach churned.

"I don't think I'm supposed to be getting married right now. I am so sorry." Sarah pulled the diamond from her finger, placed it in Brandon's hand, and folded his fingers around it.

Brandon couldn't even find the words to protest her statements. As hard as he tried to hold back, he felt a big tear fall from his cheek. Brandon turned his back to Sarah and faced the driveway. As he heard Barbara and Gus counting down the last five seconds before the ball dropped,

He turned to Sarah, kissed her on the head and said the only thing he could think of, "Happy New Year, Sarah. I love you more than you'll ever know." Brandon dropped his head in defeat and dragged himself away.

Sarah hadn't moved. Passing by her on the walk, he heard her whisper, "I love you too, Brandon. I just can't be with you right now. God, I hope I heard you right because I just let a really great guy go!"

Oh my goodness! What has Sarah done? Guilt is a beast and when we think it's gone, it's really not. Brandon and Sarah's story is not done. If you want to find out what happens with them, read Moving On. It takes place five years after this story. Will a grown up Lily and an African mission trip bring Brandon and Sarah together? Keep reading for a preview of Moving On.

HOW ABOUT A REVIEW?

YOUR FEEDBACK IS VALUABLE, so please consider sharing your thoughts. This will help other readers discover this book and my other works.

Thank you from the bottom of my heart for reading and reviewing my book(s).

Amazon

Goodreads

Bookbub

Acknowledgements

"And whatever you do, whether in word or deed, do it all in the name of the Lord Jesus, giving thanks to God the Father through him." ~ Colossians 3:17

This book would not have been possible without the Good Lord's. It may be cliché, but I believe it wholeheartedly!

For a book of this magnitude to come together it takes a lot of time and many dedicated people to ensure the success of the book. First, I must thank my dear husband, Donnie, for enduring many extra long days and nights with our daughter during the editing process. Next, my editor's husband, Pete, for enduring long work days and extended evenings with his kids in order for Deidre to work one-on-one with me to help this be one of my great works.

Deidre, thank you immensely for the dedication you put into this book with me. Even though there were some extremely long nights, they were filled with fun, laughter, and worship. Ever since we met, you have pushed me to grow spiritually, and I hope this book is an indication of how I've grown. Through this process, I began to evolve into the writer I aspire to be. Your presence in my life is irreplaceable—you are my best friend.

To my IG/Bookstagram friends—you are the best community and I am blessed to be a part of it. Thank you for welcoming me with open arms and being there to support me.

To all BETA and ARC readers—you are invaluable! THANK YOU for your support. Being an indie author is hard, and your support is invaluable.

To all my readers—saying, "Thank you" is just not enough! With all the possibilities you have, you read one of my books and it's an honor. Without you, I wouldn't be an author. Thank you for bringing me along into your life. Until we meet again...

ABOUT THE AUTHOR

KAREN TUCCI, A PUBLIC school teacher by profession, now tutors writing students online and homeschools her two children while she writes fun closed-door romance, she hopes everyone likes to read.

A native of Maine, she has trekked miles of the Pine Tree State and visited countless others. It is through her life experiences that the basis for her romance stories develop. One of her favorite things to say when out adventuring is, "...that is definitely going in my next book!"

Connect with Karen:

https://www.trueheartromance.com
Instagram
Goodreads
Bookbub
Amazon

EXCERPT FROM MOVING ON

As SARAH BOARDED THE plane for the final leg of this ridiculously long flight, an incoming call from Lily appeared on the screen. "Hey, Girlie. I'm settling into my seat now."

"Yay. I can't wait to see you. Kurt and I will pick you up at the airport instead of a team leader. Mom, there's been a bit of a mix-up, and you'll have to—"

"—Ladies and gentlemen, this is your captain speaking." Sarah pulled the phone away from her ear. "We've been asked to wait a little longer as a group of people from a delayed connecting flight are getting their tickets scanned for this flight. It is the final trip of the day to Mt. Kilimanjaro airport. I appreciate your patience."

Putting the phone back to her ear, Sarah sighed. "We've been delayed. We're waiting on a group of late arrivals."

"That's okay, Mom. I'm sure it will be worth it."

What did that mean? Sarah didn't like her daughter's tone. As a teenager, she'd always known when Lily was up to something. Her pitch got an octave higher, and her singsong tone was extra sweet, just like now. What did she know that Sarah didn't? Sarah was afraid to ask.

"See you in a few hours. Love you, Mom." She hung up quickly.

A gazillion questions ran through Sarah's mind. Namely, what were Lily and Kurt conjuring up? Hopefully, there wasn't anything wrong with her volunteering. Why wouldn't the leader be meeting her at the airport? She wouldn't worry about that right now. Instead, Sarah would get some shut-eye and pray that no one sat beside her on this flight. On her trip here, she had to listen to the grumpy man next to her complaining nonstop about the child behind him while the mother tried her hardest to keep the child quiet. Sarah stood and shut the overhead compartment, hoping no one would stuff anything else in there with her carry-on.

Dealing with adults was definitely more challenging than with children. Maybe that's why Sarah enjoyed teaching, both in the brick-and-mortar style and online. The younger ones, like the one on the plane, were her favorite. They were honest and genuine. Sarah could teach them new things, and their eyes would light up. Adults were hard to read, standoffish, and too secretive. She knew that all too well. In fact, she had been accused of being all those things at one time or another.

"Ah." Settled in her seat, Sarah tried to get comfortable for the last three and a half hours of this thirty-one-hour trip. Exhaustion raided her body. She'd never understood why flights flew past people's destinations to layover for hours before flying back to their desired destination.

Being in Qatar hadn't bothered Sarah, but as she squeezed her eyes shut, she was happy to relax in her first-class seat. The spacious seat felt like a big puffy cloud on her back and legs, dismissing whatever problem might await her at the mission site. Her eyes slowly shut.

"Woo hoo!" Roars and cheers startled Sarah. They were still sitting on the tarmac. *How long has it been?* Sarah heard the commotion in the plane's general seating area, announcing the late passengers' arrival.

Finally, we can get moving. Sarah looked at her watch – fifteen minutes past the scheduled departure time. She'd never heard of planes waiting around for people, but she wasn't a frequent flier either. She wasn't complaining, though. If she had been part of this group, she'd want people to wait for her. Elated that they'd leave soon, she repositioned herself to return to la-la land.

She let her mind wander as she stared out the miniature window. Moments later, the flight attendant pulled her from her thoughts. "Right here, sir." The blonde stewardess stood, pointing to the empty seat next to Sarah. "Enjoy your flight."

Sarah's eyes caught sight of the most handsome man alive. Her jaw hinged open, and her mouth instantly dried up like the Sahara. This woman lost all control. Her rapid heartbeat and breathing grew exponentially. Sarah shivered. Her clammy arms and hands had her wishing for a sweatshirt. Then, like a drop thrill ride, her heart plummeted into her stomach. *Where are those little barf bags?* She desperately needed one, as her nerves were getting the best of her. As the man approached the seat, time seemed to stand still. *I had said my prayers this morning; maybe He was in a joking mood. No, this is a dream, right, Lord?* Sarah pinched herself. *Nope.* She was fully awake and unprepared. Fear and excitement ransacked her body.

Maybe all her daydreams were finally coming to fruition. Maybe his proximity would force her to do what she should have done years ago. Maybe, just maybe, God was answering her prayers.

"H-Hi Brandon."

www.ingramcontent.com/pod-product-compliance
Lightning Source LLC
Chambersburg PA
CBHW032312310726
48973CB00008B/2614